D0055997

# WHITEOUT

# HUNTED: BOOK THREE

# WHITEOUT

Walter Sorrells

DUTTON CHILDREN'S BOOKS

DUTTON CHILDREN'S BOOKS
*A division of Penguin Young Readers Group*

Published by the Penguin Group
Penguin Group (USA) Inc., 375 Hudson Street, New York, New York 10014, U.S.A.
Penguin Group (Canada), 90 Eglinton Avenue East, Suite 700, Toronto, Ontario M4P 2Y3,
Canada (a division of Pearson Penguin Canada Inc.)
Penguin Books Ltd, 80 Strand, London WC2R 0RL, England
Penguin Ireland, 25 St Stephen's Green, Dublin 2, Ireland
(a division of Penguin Books Ltd)
Penguin Group (Australia), 250 Camberwell Road, Camberwell, Victoria 3124,
Australia (a division of Pearson Australia Group Pty Ltd)
Penguin Books India Pvt Ltd, 11 Community Centre, Panchsheel Park,
New Delhi - 110 017, India
Penguin Group (NZ), 67 Apollo Drive, Rosedale, North Shore 0632, New Zealand
(a division of Pearson New Zealand Ltd.)
Penguin Books (South Africa) (Pty) Ltd, 24 Sturdee Avenue, Rosebank,
Johannesburg 2196, South Africa
Penguin Books Ltd, Registered Offices: 80 Strand, London WC2R 0RL, England

This book is a work of fiction. Names, characters, places, and incidents are either the product
of the author's imagination or are used fictitiously, and any resemblance to actual persons,
living or dead, business establishments, events, or locales is entirely coincidental.

The publisher does not have any control over and does not assume any responsibility for
author or third-party websites or their content.

CIP DATA IS AVAILABLE.

Published in the United States by Dutton Children's Books,
a division of Penguin Young Readers Group
345 Hudson Street, New York, New York 10014
www.penguin.com/youngreaders

Printed in USA | First Edition
ISBN 978-0-525-42141-2 | 10 9 8 7 6 5 4 3 2 1

*To Mom and Dad*

WHITEOUT

# PROLOGUE

**ALONE.**

Completely alone. That's how it feels when you're in a whiteout blizzard. You can't hear anything but the wind and the crunching of your feet on the snow. You can't see anything but snow. The trees, the fields, the barns, the silos, the John Deere tractors, the sky, the wheeling blackbirds—all gone.

They call it a whiteout. But really, when a true blizzard comes on in Minnesota, it's more of a *gray*out. The snow is so heavy that it blots out the light. So it seems like there's nothing in the universe but you and the gray swirling snow.

Welcome to Snow World. In Snow World, there's nothing but snow. Snow above you, snow below you, snow all around you.

They find people dead, frozen in the snow after white-out storms. Sometimes a person will die fifteen, twenty feet from a building where they could have found shelter. But the snow's falling so heavily they can't even see it. They just sit down and freeze to death.

So, needless to say, I shouldn't have been out in Snow World. The problem was, I had to find something that was in the silo. I had to. And in the meantime, the killer was chasing me. If he caught up to me before I found what was in the silo . . . well, then I was in *real* trouble.

I staggered blindly through the snow. It was six degrees. My lungs felt like they were full of needles. My gloves were thin. My feet and fingers were freezing.

But the worst feeling was the sensation of being alone. When you're in Snow World, there's nobody else. I felt more alone than I'd ever felt in my life. Even when my mom disappeared on my sixteenth birthday—I didn't feel like this.

The snow was sticking to my hat, to my hair, to my coat. The normal world had disappeared. Nothing left but snow. My shoes crunched. The snow swirled. I was alone. It was all on me now. Just me, just Chass, just this lonely, freezing sixteen-year-old girl. And the snow.

*Keep moving,* I thought. *Just keep moving. You don't want to end up like her.* I saw a flash in my mind, a woman lying in the snow, arms and legs twisted, her blood staining the whiteness.

The snow.

# ONE

**I MUST HAVE** heard the gunshot. But I didn't really notice it. In rural Minnesota, people are always shooting guns. So you don't really think about it.

Plus, snow muffles sound.

In Minnesota, they're always telling you how they never let bad weather stop them from doing anything. Get a Minnesotan wound up on the subject of weather and they'll go on and on and on about how they play football games in twenty below zero snowstorms and all this junk. So I figured, okay, my performance in the gym at the high school was going to go on, come heck or high water (people look at you funny if you say "hell" in the town of Greenville, Minnesota).

I mean, it was only like twenty-five degrees outside. Which is nothing for Minnesota. But the snow? I'd never seen snow like this before in my life. There had been snow, then freezing rain, then more snow. The few cars on the road had been sliding all over the place.

And then came the whiteout.

You literally couldn't see anything. *Nothing.* Just snow. But Mom and I were living in a little apartment over Krieghoff Yamaha, right smack across the street from the church. So I figured, hey, this is Minnesota. The show must go on. I'd told Mr. Osmund, the school principal, that I was going to do my sound check at noon, even though the show wasn't until Saturday night. So I grabbed my guitar and started walking straight into the tangle of snow.

Eventually I bumped into the school. I mean, more or less literally. I just put my left hand on the wall and kept walking, my guitar case bumping against my leg, until I found a door. It was locked.

So I walked around until I found another door.

Locked. Same with the door to the lunchroom. Same with the door to the band room. That only left one more door—the door to the gym. Which was where I was supposed to play anyway.

By the time I reached the door, my fingers were frozen and I was feeling kind of weird and queasy. It was the alone thing. I mean, until you've been in a whiteout, you just don't know what it feels like. There's no noise or anything, and you can't see squat. It's like you're floating in space.

Anyway, so finally I got to the door of the band room. And it was locked, too. No note. No lights on inside. Nobody waiting outside to find out what was going on. Nothing.

Which is when I realized that all this "Minnesotans never stop for bad weather" stuff was total baloney (to use the word preferred by people in Greenville . . . as opposed to the word I probably would have used in, say, San Francisco). Or at least, it was baloney when it came to whiteout blizzards. I guess in Minnesota, you have to be realists about the weather. Cold is no joke. Snow is no joke. A whiteout? *Definitely* no joke.

So, probably everybody in Greenville knew the secret postscript to "Minnesotans never stop for bad weather." Which was: ". . . except for whiteouts. In which case you'd be a total moron to do anything but sit in your house and wait until the whiteout's over."

Now that I knew, I felt like an idiot.

A scared idiot. Because I wasn't sure that I knew where Broad Street was anymore. And if I couldn't find Broad Street, I couldn't get home. I could end up being one of those peoplesicles lying in the snow ten feet from a nice warm house.

As I was standing next to the school, trying to figure out what to do, I looked out at what, I guess, was the parking lot. Though it just looked like more gray, whirling nothingness. Then there was a sort of lull in the storm. Not a real break. But just enough that I could see thirty or forty feet instead of fifteen.

That's when I saw him. A man. He wore a heavy coat with the hood up and a pair of dark sunglasses. So I couldn't make out his face. But I could tell he was looking at me.

"Hey!" I yelled. "Can you—"

He turned away from me. Quickly. Like somebody who had not wanted to be seen.

And then the snow drove a wedge between us and he disappeared from view.

"Hey!" I shouted. "You think you could help me? I need to—"

My voice felt all soft and squashy and pressed down in the snow.

"Hey!"

But the man was gone.

Did I mention how alone you feel in a whiteout? I ran toward the man. I mean, I knew it was stupid. I knew the second that I got away from the school, I wouldn't be able to see anything. And then I might get lost.

"Hey!" I yelled. "Hey!"

*Wham!*

Next thing I knew, I was facedown in the snow. I'd stumbled over something.

I pushed myself to my knees, felt around for my guitar. I couldn't lose my beloved Takamine. I would *totally* freak out then! My guitar was my life.

My hand closed around something. For a second I thought it was the handle of my guitar case. But then I realized no, it was something else. It felt like—

I went rigid for a moment. Then I turned to look at what I was touching. There was just enough visibility to see: it was a hand. A thin, female hand. I sat up sharply.

A woman. I had tripped over . . . a *woman*! A

woman who was lying facedown in the snow. She wore a heavy down coat. But no hat, no gloves.

"Ma'am?" I said. My voice trembled. "Ma'am? Are you okay?"

No answer.

I jumped off of her, rolled her over. It was an old lady with white hair. I recognized her immediately. It was Miss Hill, the music teacher from Lars G. Dahlgren High, the school I attended.

A red stain had seeped out into the snow where her face had been.

In the middle of her forehead was a small round hole. Miss Hill was dead. Like I said earlier—I must have heard the gunshot. But I don't remember it.

I screamed. When I ran out of breath, I sucked in air. Then I screamed again.

The one thing they always say in Minnesota about whiteouts is that you can't panic. You have to stay calm. You have to have a plan. You can't just go running blindly into the snow. You have to—

I jumped up and ran blindly into the snow.

# TWO

**WHEN MOM AND** I moved to Greenville, Minnesota, last month, it seemed like such a relief. After living in San Francisco, Greenville seemed so peaceful, so calm, so orderly. No hustle, no bustle, no weirdos. Just a town full of straight-ahead, earnest, decent Midwestern people.

My best friend, Katie, says this is an illusion. She says that under the surface, people in Greenville are the weirdest people in the world. Maybe she's right. But lemme tell you . . . Katie's never been to San Francisco. I could tell you some stuff that happened to me out there that . . .

Well. Like they say, that's another story.

Anyway, the first day I walked into Dahlgren High, Katie walked right up to me as I came in the front door and said, "Hi, my name's Katie Blaufuss. *Blaufuss* means 'blue foot' in German. Isn't that totally bizarre? You must be Carla Darden. I heard there was a new girl! I can see you and me are gonna be best friends."

"Hi," I said. "Yeah, I'm . . . uh . . . Carla. But everybody calls me Chass."

"Chass! How'd you get that from Carla?"

"Long story," I said.

Katie Blaufuss was a large girl. Not large fat, but large in every other way. She had large eyes and large lips and black hair that went boinging out in every direction. She was very tall. She was dressed all in black with high black boots and long black fingernails. She had about a zillion rings and studs sticking out of her face. One in her lip, one in her nose, a couple in her eyebrows, and tons in her ears. And you could just tell that she had a large personality, too—the kind of person who could carry on a conversation with a wall.

Katie grabbed my arm and said, "Come on, let's go

13

see Miss Hill. I heard you were a musician. When I heard you were coming, I went ahead and got you signed up for all your classes. First period's Band."

"But—"

"This way!" Katie said, dragging me down the hallway. "Better hustle. Miss Hill's gonna give us a raft of doodie flop if we're tardy."

I'd been in Greenville for precisely twelve hours at that point. Mom and I had rolled into town the previous evening, checked into the Fisherman's Haven Motel, eaten dinner at the Greenville Diner, and gone to bed. Period. And already, apparently, everybody in town knew our life story. Or, what passed for our life story. Which is actually something very different.

See, my mom and I have been on the run all my life. I won't go into the whole thing, but there's this guy named Kyle Van Epps who has been chasing Mom since the day I was born. If he catches us, we're both dead. I've lived in about twenty different towns in my life, and I've had about twenty different names. So when we get to a new town, we have a "life story"—Mom calls it The Legend—that we tell everybody. But it's not true, none of it.

There are things you can't change about yourself, though—things that have to be incorporated into The

Legend. I'm sixteen. I play guitar. I sing. I have blond hair. I'm five foot four. I wear a C-cup bra and I suck at volleyball. These are things you can't fake. Well, I mean I guess you can stuff your bra and dye your hair. But I'm not that kind of person. I'm more the keep-it-real type. I had a friend in Alabama who used to say, "You wouldn't be so into keeping it real if you had mouse-brown hair and a flat chest." Which might be true. But I guess I'll never know. You are who you are, right?

But more on that later.

I guess somebody must have heard me talking about music at the Greenville Diner the night before. And somehow, within the next twelve hours, the information got to Katie Blaufuss.

And so here I was, walking into the band room at Lars G. Dahlgren High School, everybody staring at me. When you change schools once or twice a year, you get used to people staring at you. Sort of. I mean, it always blows—having people stare at you? But you realize after a while that it's not personal. It's just what happens. When you come into a place and you're new, you mess up the old rhythms, make people feel strange and uncomfortable. I don't know why, but that's how people are.

"Ah!" the gray-haired lady standing on the podium in the front of the class said. "You must be Carla Darden. Welcome to Band. What instrument do you play?"

"Uh . . . well, actually, I guess somebody got their wires crossed," I said. "I'm a guitar player."

"The guitar is not a band instrument," Miss Hill said, smiling broadly. She was very thin and leathery, with that crinkly kind of face you get after you've smoked a billion cigarettes. She wore little half-glasses around her neck on a chain made from paper clips. "So I guess you'll have to play something else. We're short a piccolo. Go back there and pick up that little black case on the shelf behind Oscar." She pointed. "Oscar's the fat boy with the tuba."

Miss Hill didn't say it in a mean way. There was just something very strong and assertive and matter-of-fact about her. I could tell she was the sort of person who, when she told people something, they pretty much did exactly what she told them to do. I had zero interest in being in the Lars G. Dahlgren marching band. Or in playing the piccolo. But you get good at reading people when you change schools every six months. I could see that arguing with Miss Hill was a total waste of time. She had made up her mind. And that was that.

"Yes, ma'am," I said.

As I went back to the shelf and picked up the small black case, Miss Hill said, "I presume you read music."

"A little." I'd taken piano lessons when I lived in Ohio. Also in Texas. I don't really read music on the guitar, but I know enough from playing piano that I can muddle through. And how hard could a piccolo be? You only played one note at a time. On guitar you can play six at a time.

"Carla," Miss Hill said, "you'll need to—"

"It's Chass, ma'am," I said. "I go by Chass. C-H-A-S-S."

Miss Hill looked at me over her little half-glasses for about fourteen seconds. She had extremely blue eyes. "Chass," she said finally. "As in Chastity."

"Yes, ma'am."

Another fourteen-second stare. "Okay, then. Chass it is . . . Now, Chass, I don't have time to waste with individual lessons at this moment. You'll need to stay after school today. I'll show you the embrasure and the fingering then. I can see just from looking at you that you'll pick it up right away."

Staying after school? Whoopee. That was right up there with playing piccolo in the marching band. But, like I say, total waste of time arguing with this lady.

"Yes, ma'am," I said.

"Cool!" Katie Blaufuss said. "Guess what the Blue Foot plays?" Katie, I would find out, referred to herself in third person all the time. But instead of calling herself Katie, she called herself the Blue Foot. She was the only one who called herself this. Everybody else called her Metalface, because of all her piercings. But, of course, I didn't know any of this yet.

"Well . . ."

"Yes!" Katie said triumphantly as she slapped the seat of the chair next to her. "Piccolo! That's so *awesome*! We are *totally* gonna be best friends!"

And that's how I became best friends with the weirdest girl in Greenville, and how I became a member of the woodwind section of the Lars G. Dahlgren High School Marching Gobblers.

# THREE

SOMEHOW I MADE it across the street through the whiteout snow. Blind luck, I guess. I slammed into a wall, felt around until I reached a door . . . and it turned out to be the building where Mom and I lived. My heart was still banging in my ribs and I had this terrible coppery taste in my mouth as I felt my way up the iron railing to the door of our house.

Mom was reading.

Without looking at me, she said, "I told you they'd

cancel the gig. Even these nuts in Minnesota know when to throw in the towel."

I just stood there inside the doorway, shaking. I couldn't seem to make myself move.

Finally she looked up. She didn't even blink. I don't know what she saw in my eyes—but she saw something.

"Get your things," she said. "We have to go."

"Don't you even want to know what happened?" I said.

But she was already opening the closet door, pulling out the two bags that we always have packed and ready. The bags contain enough clothes for a week, along with the props for our legend. Every legend requires props. A couple of photos, a yearbook, a souvenir or two, a few things like that.

"No," I said. "It's too dangerous out there."

"We have to go," she said.

"I'm telling you, if we get in the car and start driving, we'll run into something. It's a straight-up whiteout."

Mom looked out the window. "My God," she said. "I didn't think it could get worse. But it has."

"I found a dead body," I said. "Miss Hill, my band teacher."

"What!" Mom said.

"Look, it didn't have anything to do with us. She's just an old lady who teaches at the high school. What could this have to do with us?"

Mom put the bags by the door. "This is bad. This is really bad." She opened the door, looked out. Snow swirled into the room. She slammed the door. "This is *so* bad."

"It's got nothing to do with—"

"You don't know that," Mom said. "And we can't take a chance."

"Mom, I'm sick of leaving every time we just get settled in to a place. I *like* this town. I'm starting to make some friends . . ."

Mom shook her head sharply. "We're not having this discussion again. As soon as the snow lets up, we're leaving."

We'd been having a running battle for years. Mom is so jumpy that she leaves towns at the drop of a hat. A hang-up phone call, a person who looked at Mom funny, a telemarketer, a car that's parked outside our house two days in a row—anything could set Mom off. My guess is we left half the places I've lived—maybe even nine out of ten of them—out of pure paranoia.

And I was sick of it. Even with that dead body lying

out there bleeding all over the snow—I still couldn't stand to leave this place.

"You can't leave me, if you can't find me," I said.

"What's that supposed to mean?" Mom had little red spots on her cheeks. She put her hands on her hips.

I wasn't really sure what I meant. Until I opened the door and walked out into the snow.

"Young lady, you get back here right this minute!"

I scrambled down the icy iron stairs as fast as I dared. When I got to the bottom and looked up, I couldn't even see the door of our apartment.

Mom's voice sounded thin and compressed. "I'm talking to you! Chass!" There was a pause. Her voice rose higher. She sounded scared now. "Chass! Chass? Where'd you go, Chass? Please, Chass, you could die out there!"

"I'll be back later," I shouted. "I have to go tell the police." Then I plunged into the gray strangeness of the storm. I was alone again. But now I felt a little better about it. I wanted to be alone. I wanted to make my own decisions. I wanted—

*Bam!*

I slammed into a giant hard lump of snow. A car

parked . . . well . . . parked somewhere. I felt around the snowy lump of metal, kept moving.

The fact was, I'd been in this kind of position once before. A guy had gotten murdered back in San Francisco. Mom had wanted to leave. I'd struck a bargain that if I could solve the crime in twenty-four hours, we wouldn't leave. As it turned out, we had to go anyway.

But I figured this time would be different. If I could just hold Mom back until the crime got solved, we could stay.

And how hard could it be to solve a murder in Greenville, Minnesota? As small as the town was, there just couldn't be that many suspects. Right?

Besides, it made me feel better. I've been around death more than a kid my age should. And one thing I've found is that if you sit around thinking about dead people, you start freaking out. Real quick. But if you find something to do, give yourself a goal, get busy on it—you don't feel quite so much like lying on your bed and crying like a baby.

I pushed on through the snow. We lived right in downtown Greenville. There wasn't much to it—but at least there were plenty of buildings. I figured just by luck I'd blunder into one of them after a while. Then I could get my bearings and start hunting for the police station.

The police station was in a former gas station about two blocks down Broad Street. As long as I headed in the right direction, I ought to be able to get there. Eventually.

As I was walking I heard a noise. A car. *What kind of idiot would be driving a car right now?* I wondered. And then I realized the noise was coming right toward me. In this visibility, they could run right over me in a heartbeat. I tried to move away from the noise. But the snow played tricks on my ears.

Suddenly the car was *right there*. I mean it was like *Star Trek,* just beaming down ten feet from where I was standing. And it was coming right toward me!

I jumped out of the way. But my feet slipped and I fell. The car was almost right on top of me. I rolled desperately to my left. And then the car was past me. It was a Beemer. The rear bumper passed so close that I felt it brush my head and almost pull off my hat.

The car disappeared into the snow. But not fast enough that I couldn't see the license plate.

CALIFORNIA.

I lay there in the snow, panting. California. That was where Kyle Van Epps was from. I scrambled to my feet. For a moment the thought occurred to me that maybe the car was actually *trying* to hit me.

No, that didn't make sense. There was no way they could have known it was me. Not in this crazy snow.

Still . . . maybe Mom was right. Maybe we *should* get out of here.

But how? I stumbled through the snow, my arms out in front of me like a blind person. And then, for a moment, I saw a ghost. Or . . . it looked like a ghost anyway.

It was a dark figure that appeared and then disappeared. But I managed to see what the ghost had in its hand. It was a gun.

"Hey!" a voice said.

I ran from the voice, tripped, sprawled in the snow.

"Hey!" the voice said again.

Then a man was standing over me, a gun in his hand.

"Don't shoot me," I whispered.

The man stared impassively down at me. Then he lifted the gun, a silver revolver with a long barrel.

"Wolves," the man said.

# FOUR

"HUH?" I LAY on the ground, trembling.

"Wolves," the man said, waggling the pistol.

"Excuse me?"

"Wolves." He held up the pistol. "I just saw wolves in the snow. A wolf can smell its prey for close to a mile." He pulled back the bottom of his heavy coat and shoved the revolver into a holster. "Better safe than sorry."

It was only then that I was able to make out the man's features.

"Just the man I'm looking for," I said with relief. It was Oswald Norgren, the chief of police.

"Oh?" Chief Norgren said. "Why's that?"

"Miss Hill," I said. "Miss Hill's been murdered."

He stared at me for a long time. Then he leaned down, grabbed my hand, and hoisted me to my feet. "You better come with me," he said.

A couple of minutes later we were sitting in the warm confines of the Greenville police station. The police chief got a cup of coffee, dumped about eight sugars and a bunch of nondairy creamer in it, then said, "Now, what's this about Miss Hill, hon?"

"Murdered," I said. "Shot in the head."

Chief Norgren was a medium-size man with sandy hair and a scraggly mustache that almost—but didn't quite—cover the scar of a harelip. He rubbed his face and squinted at me with one eye. "Ya want to run that by me again?" he said. Chief Norgren had about the strongest Minnesota accent I'd ever heard.

"She's lying over there in the snow," I said. "In the parking lot of the high school."

"Huh," he said. Then he rubbed his face again. "Ya wouldn't be playing with me, wouldya? 'Cause that wouldn't be so funny."

"Do I look like I'm joking?" I said. I held up my trembling left hand.

"No," Chief Norgren said. He rubbed his face some more. He seemed thoughtful and kind of scared at the same time. He didn't have that usual police tough-guy look. He just looked like a normal guy. Kind of on the soft and weak end of normal, actually. "No, I guess ya don't."

Then he stood up, put on his hat, got out his gun and a big roll of yellow plastic tape that said POLICE on it. "We're gonna use the tape to keep a trail so we can find our way back," he said. "Show me where she's at." Then he pushed the door open, tied the end of the tape to the door handle, and started walking into the snow. I hurried after him, running my hand along the crime-scene tape. We walked and walked, the roll of tape getting smaller and smaller. I don't know why, but it scared me, seeing the tape going away like that.

Finally we found ourselves next to the sign for the school. If we'd gotten there ten minutes later, it probably would have been covered by snow. Still, it took us another fifteen minutes to find Miss Hill.

"Over here," I said. My heart was pounding as we got closer to where I knew she would be.

"Gosh," Chief Norgren said, looking down at Miss Hill's body. She lay half covered in snow. "Good goshamighty."

He just stood there for a long time, staring. I kept waiting for him to do something. But he seemed kind of frozen.

"So I guess you should put tape around her?" I said.

"What?" he said, looking up suddenly and blinking.

"Crime-scene tape. Aren't you supposed to put crime-scene tape around her so nobody will mess with her?"

The chief stared at the roll in his hand like he'd never seen crime-scene tape before. "Uh, yeah," he said. "I guess I better, huh?" He smiled at me halfheartedly. "Ain't never had a murder here before. I'm a little . . . I'm a little . . . well, I'm not totally sure what I need to do." He sighed. "I guess I better get the BCA out here."

"What's that?"

"State police." He kept staring at Miss Hill. "Dang. She taught music to me when I was a kid. I played the trombone, if ya can believe that." Then he turned back to me. "Ya don't need to be looking at that no more."

"I'll help you with the crime-scene tape," I said. "I don't want to go back through this snow by myself."

Chief Norgren nodded. "Yeah. Yeah. Okay, yeah, I guess that makes sense." He was looking more and more freaked out by the minute.

We shuffled around in the snow looking for things to hang the crime-scene tape off of and Chief Norgren kept telling me about the various ways in which he had displayed incompetence as a trombone player.

Finally we got done. Then we followed the tape back to the police station.

"What are you going to do?" I said as we walked in and took our coats off and stomped on the floor to get the snow off our shoes.

"Nothing I can do," he said. He kept blinking and swallowing. "Call the BCA and wait."

"You're not going to investigate."

He blinked and swallowed, blinked and swallowed. "Investigate?"

"Yeah, like, I don't know—interview people? See if there are footprints in the snow? Look for . . . like . . . fingerprints?" He looked at me blankly. "I mean, can't you do *something*?"

"'Scuse me, hon." Chief Norgren hustled back through a doorway behind his desk. I caught a glimpse of a sink and half of a toilet before the door slammed shut. After a few seconds I heard retching noises.

I was getting a pretty strong feeling that Chief Nor-gren was in over his head. *Way* over his head!

When Chief Norgren came back out, he said, "I'm sorry ya had to hear that, hon. I'm afraid I might be in just, oh, just a little tiny bit over my head here." He smiled weakly. "Ya know what I mean?"

"I do," I said.

Chief Norgren blinked. Then he swallowed. "*Oh,* boy!" he said. Then he went back in the bathroom and made throw-up noises for a while—though I don't imagine he had much left to throw up by then.

When he came out the second time, his face was all pale. He sat down on a box next to his desk, took a deep breath, pulled a little notebook out of his desk, and said, "Lemme get your full name, hon."

I told him my latest fake name, which was Carla Justine Darden. Then I told him everything that had happened to me, everything I'd seen. Which was not much.

"You recognize this man you seen over there?" he said.

I shook my head. "No. Honestly? It could even have been a woman for all I could tell," I said. "They had a big coat on and a hood. But they saw me, I'll tell you that."

The chief scribbled in his pad for a while.

"Heard an outta-town fella checked into the Fisherman's Haven last night. Here it ain't even trout season yet." He cleared his throat. "Kinda spooky-looking character, they said."

"Where was he from?" I said, my heart doing a flip in my chest.

Chief Norgren squinted thoughtfully. "Believe I heard he was from somewhere out west. California, maybe?"

California. Same as the car that almost hit me.

"Anything else?" he said finally.

"Did you really see a wolf out there?" I said.

He nodded.

"The reason I ask," I said. "Before the state police get here, it would kind of be bad if some wolf dragged Miss Hill off and ate her."

He hopped up out of his chair. "Dang it!" he said. "I didn't even thinka that." Then he gave me a sharp look. "Ya seem to be thinking a heck of a lot straighter than me. If I didn't know better, I'd of thought ya'd been through something like this before."

I didn't say anything.

He put his coat back on, drew his gun, and got

ready to walk back out into the snow. "Wolves!" he said. "Goshdangit, I *hate* wolves!"

Then the door opened, the snow swirled, and he was gone.

I sat for a minute, trying to think what to do next. Finally I checked under the desk, found another roll of crime-scene tape, went out the front door, and started unrolling the tape, leaving a trail as I tried to find my way back down the street to where Mom and I lived.

It seemed like it took forever. But eventually I got there. It wasn't our apartment that I was looking for, though. It was the building underneath. A big sign outside said:

KRIEGHOFF YAMAHA

ATVS—MOTORCYCLES—SNOWMOBILES

NOBODY UNDERSELLS KRIEGHOFF!

I knocked on the front door of the Yamaha dealership. I knew Mr. Krieghoff, so I was hoping he might loan me a snowmobile. But the door was locked. So I followed the wall around to the back of the building.

My mom and I have our problems. Sometimes I get really mad at her about this or that. But I have to say, in general, she's the coolest mom you could ever ask for. I mean, how many mothers do you know who teach their daughters how to drive when they're eleven years old? She had said, "One day I might be hurt and you might need to be able to drive in order to save us." So even though I actually still don't have a license, I know how to drive. She used to take me out and teach me driving tricks. How to skid, how to brake into turns and accelerate out of them without wrecking, stuff like that.

I mention that only as an example. She's also taught me a lot of other weird stuff. Like, oh, how to hot-wire a car. Or a motorcycle.

There was a row of snowmobiles lined up behind Krieghoff Yamaha. I figured, hey, Mr. Krieghoff wouldn't mind if I borrowed one. The one on the end was a crappy-looking used machine with a big gash over the gas tank, so I didn't feel too bad about borrowing it. I mean, I felt bad . . . but not *bad* bad.

Still, my heart was beating hard and my palms were sweating, even in the twenty-five-degree weather.

As I quickly found out, if you can hot-wire a car or a motorcycle, hot-wiring a snowmobile is child's play. I yanked out the wire harness, found the right wires, took off my gloves long enough to touch them together. There was a brief spark, then the engine roared to life.

I pulled my gloves back on and leaned forward to look at the controls. I'd never driven a snowmobile, so I had no idea what I was doing.

"Hey!" A voice from behind me cut through the air.

Then a pair of rough hands grabbed me and yanked me off the snowmobile.

# FIVE

**MY HEART STARTED** racing even faster than it had been before. I was lying on the snow staring up into the air.

"What in the heck you think you're doing, boy?" the man said. I recognized him then. It was Mr. Krieghoff, the old guy who owned the Yamaha store underneath where we lived.

"Uh . . . for one thing, I'm not a boy," I said, pushing back my hood so he could see my face. "And, uh, I was just borrowing a snowmobile."

"The heck you are!" He narrowed his eyes, bent over me. "Hey, you're Ellen's kid, aren't you?" Ellen Darden was the name my mom was going by while we lived in Greenville.

"I can explain!" I said. "Miss Hill, the music teacher . . . she's been murdered."

"Bull." Mr. Krieghoff's eyebrows went up. Mr. Krieghoff was actually our landlord. Every time Mom went down to pay the rent, Mr. Krieghoff would make a pass at her. He was married and a deacon at one of the churches in town—but that didn't seem to stop him from hitting on my mother at every opportunity. In fairness to the old guy, my mother is pretty hot for a forty-year-old lady. But still . . .

"I'm serious. She's lying over there in the snow. In the parking lot of the high school."

Mr. Krieghoff kept staring skeptically at me. He was probably about seventy years old, but he was still a very handsome guy. In a shifty sort of way. "*Evangeline* Hill?" he said.

"Yes," I said. "I think that's her first name."

Mr. Krieghoff's jaw worked. "That's impossible," he snapped. "I just saw her yesterday."

"We can't drive because of the blizzard," I said, "so I needed to borrow the snowmobile."

"For *what*?" he snapped.

"Uh . . . I have to . . . uh . . . investigate."

"You do, huh? You Sherlock Holmes? Huh? You that red-haired jerkoff from that TV show? *CSI*? Huh? Yeah? Huh? Huh? You the *CSI* guy? Huh?"

"No, but . . ."

"Yeah, didn't think so. Now get up and turn off that sled. I'm sure Chief Norgren doesn't need your help."

"Actually, he's kind of busy throwing up and scaring away wolves," I said. "I don't think investigating the murder is high on his list right now."

Mr. Krieghoff kept chewing on his gum, his jaws working hard. "That doesn't mean you got permission to steal my goddarn snowmobile," he said.

"Look, the smart thing would be—"

"Smart?" he said. "Are you smart enough to spell *juvenile hall*?"

I stood back up and made a big show of dusting the snow off my pants. My heart was whacking away in my chest. If Mr. Krieghoff weren't such a jerk, I might have just turned off the snowmobile and gone back inside. But then he gave me this cheesy smile, reached over, and started gently brushing the snow off my face. Talk about creepy!

"Are you smart enough to spell *inappropriate touching*?" I said.

Then I hopped on the snowmobile and gunned the engine. The snowmobile jerked forward. In about a second, Mr. Krieghoff had been swallowed by the snow.

"Get your pretty little fanny back here!" he shouted. He was yelling more stuff as I drove away. But the sound got lost pretty quickly in the growl of the motor.

I don't know why, but I started laughing after that. I laughed so hard I finally had to stop the snowmobile. Even though I had this strange sick feeling in the pit of my stomach, I just kept laughing and laughing and laughing. Honestly, I don't know what was so funny. I just couldn't help myself.

Then I started feeling alone again. The gray snow surrounded me and the wind was howling, and the world had receded. I knew I had to stop laughing and find the place I was aiming for.

So I put the snowmobile in gear again and started driving—veeeeeerrrrry slowly—down the road. Every now and then I would bump into something. There's no telling what I was hitting. Parked cars, street signs, mailboxes, frozen dinosaurs? I couldn't tell you. All I can say for sure is that every time I hit something, I'd just back up, start moving again.

If there was anything visible that I could use as a marker of where I was, I'd file it away in my head. Once I saw a flowerpot with plastic flowers in it. Another time, the sign for the Zinnershine School of Ballet. Another time a giant holly bush at the corner of Broad and Center (that one *hurt*!). It was enough to know I was moving in the right direction.

Finally I arrived at my destination—the Fisherman's Haven Motel. Once I got there, it took me about three tries to find the office. Finally I rammed the snowmobile right into the front door of the motel, backed up just enough that I could still make out where the door was, and walked in.

A girl sat at the front desk watching *The 40-Year-Old Virgin* on TV. I recognized her from school. She was a junior named Justine Chaudry. Other than her geeky brother, she was the only Indian kid at our school. She turned and looked at me like I had just fallen through the ceiling out of the sky. She was impossibly beautiful and supposedly the bitchiest girl in the whole school—though I didn't really know her.

"Are you *insane*?" she said.

"Excuse me?" I said.

"You could totally die out there on a day like this. Why aren't you at home?"

"It's kind of a special situation," I said. "I don't know if you know me, but—"

"Yeah," she said. "You're that singer."

"I actually think of myself more as a guitar player," I said.

She looked back at the TV. It was the part where the guy was getting his chest waxed. "Oh, that's so gross!" she said. "That's disgusting."

I could see into the office behind the desk. There were about a million pictures of Justine in her cheerleader outfit hanging on the wall. Zero pictures of her geeky brother.

"Anyway . . ." I said.

"You want to buy some candy bars?" she said. "We're raising money for the big cheerleading thingy down in the Cities." There was a box of candy bars sitting on the counter with yet another picture of Justine in her cheerleader outfit, holding up her pom-poms and looking just totally jammed with team spirit. The candy bars were three bucks a pop. Which seemed a little high to me.

"I thought this late in the year you'd be done," I said.

"Summer cheering," she said disdainfully—as though anybody who wasn't aware of the summer cheerleading season was pretty much as lame as it was possible for a human to be. "We got plain or cashew or raisin."

"I don't have any money on me," I said. Then I cleared my throat. "Look, I heard you guys had a man from out of town staying here."

She looked at me and then curled her lip. "Dude, we're a freakin' motel. Everybody who stays here is from out of town."

"Okay, yeah, but this guy, I heard, was from California."

She shrugged, looked back at the TV, and made a long-drawn-out gagging noise. The actor was screaming as they stripped more hair off his chest.

"Um," I said, "do you have this guy's name or something?"

Justine Chaudry tossed her glistening black hair and blew a very large bubble. "Lot of people don't realize it, but owning a motel is like being a priest or whatever. Confidentiality is sacred."

"Is that why you were telling everybody at lunch about what those people were doing last month in the honeymoon suite?"

"That's different," she said, popping the bubble. "They were making a public nuisance."

"Oh," I said. "Well, then . . ."

She blew another bubble.

"Anyway, look, here's the thing . . . Miss Hill's been murdered."

That got her attention. Her mouth hung open. I could see the wad of gum on her tongue. "Murdered!"

I nodded. "Shot. In the face."

"Oh. My. God." She blinked. Then it was like a curtain came down over her face. "Still, I can't tell you about that guy." She took one of the candy bars out of the box and started running her long, red fingernail down the wrapper.

"What if I bought a candy bar?" I said.

The actor was still screaming.

"Ow," said Justine, her eyes not leaving the screen. "Wouldn't it be disgusting to have chest hair?"

"Okay, three," I said. "Three candy bars."

"Five."

"I'll have to pay you on Monday."

"Done." Justine tapped the keys on her computer, turned the screen around so I could see. "He's kinda cute," she said. "John Smith. From L.A."

"John *Smith*?" I said. It said he was staying in room 114. Otherwise there was no address or any other information shown on the screen. "Come on! You don't ask for ID?"

"He paid cash," Justine said, shrugging.

"What's he look like?"

"Big. Black. Scary. Sunglasses. He said he was in the music business."

The music business. That was the business that Kyle Van Epps was in. "Did he have a gun?"

"A gun? You think he—" She swallowed.

"I don't know," I said. "I don't know why somebody would come all the way out from California to shoot a high school teacher from a small town in Minnesota."

Justine still looked nervous.

"I'm sure it's a coincidence," I said.

Justine looked apprehensively out the window. "What if he's like a serial killer or something?"

"Really, I wouldn't worry about that."

Justine switched off the TV as the actor on the TV ran out of the room screaming. "I'm kinda freaking out," she said.

"So can I take my candy bars now?" I said.

Justine nodded distractedly. "There's no cashew left," she said. "Only raisin."

"Raisin!" I hate raisins. I sighed. "I don't suppose there's any way I could get into his room?"

Justine made a face at me.

"Just asking." I walked to the door. The bell tinkled as I opened it.

"Oh," Justine said, "by the way, I forgot to mention . . ."

"Mention what?"

"The guy? John Smith?" She pulled a long string of gum out of her mouth. "He showed me a picture of you. Asked if I knew you."

I felt something cold run up my spine. So Mom was right after all. We needed to get out of here. I looked out at the swirling snow. The problem was, the blizzard was still going, full whiteout. No way we could leave. "What did you tell him?" I said.

"Duh. I told him where you lived. How should I know he was a serial killer?"

My heart started pounding. I jumped onto the snowmobile. I had to get home immediately. I had to warn Mom!

I started the engine, gunned the throttle, and took off down the road. Well . . . at least I *thought* it was the road. I'd gone about a hundred yards (I guess—it's a

45

little hard to tell!) when I realized that I could have been driving through somebody's backyard for all I knew. I should have just called from the motel.

I slowed down to a crawl and started looking for something that would tell me where I was. When nearly a foot of snow has fallen, though, pretty much everything that you see just looks like a big snowy blob looming out of the grayness. That blob could be a car or a bush or a hibernating bear. Who would know?

So when I slammed into the big blob in the middle of what I imagined to be Broad Street, I wasn't sure at all what it was. All I could tell was that my snowmobile suddenly came to a screeching halt and I went flying over the handlebars and over the blob and into the grayness. My snowmobile must have turned off in the crash because I couldn't hear it anymore. In fact, I couldn't hear anything but the wind.

"Hello!" I called. "Hello! Anybody out there?"

No answer. I wasn't really hurt—the snow broke my fall—but I was a little shaken up. I stood, brushed the snow off my coat, and began staggering around looking for the snowmobile. I didn't find it. What I did find was the front window of Wiesener's Sporting Goods. I knew that it was about two blocks down from where we lived. So I just put my hand on the front of the building and started walking.

Within five minutes, I was home. My stomach clenched up when I saw several sets of footprints on the snow leading up and down the stairs to our apartment. Had the man from the hotel beaten me home? I ran up the stairs, threw open the front door. My heart was suddenly pounding.

"Mom!" I shouted. "Mom, are you here?"

There was no answer. I closed the door and began moving as silently as I could through the apartment. I paused in the kitchen to grab a butcher knife. Then I went creeping around the house, holding up the butcher knife like that guy in *Psycho,* my heart thudding around in my chest. My bedroom. Empty. Mom's room. Empty. The bathroom. The two closets . . .

"Mom?" I called one last, pointless time. We live in a small apartment. It took about thirty seconds to search every nook and cranny. She just wasn't there.

I stood in the middle of the apartment trying not to panic. But no matter how I thought about it, I couldn't come up with a good scenario. Mom and I have been on the run all our lives. Some guy from California had showed up in this little town looking for us. A woman lay dead in a parking lot not more than a hundred yards from where I stood. And now Mom was gone.

There was no good ending to this movie.

As I was standing there trying to figure out what to do, I heard a loud noise.

*BOOM. BOOM. BOOM.*

It was someone banging on the door. I grabbed my guitar—the only possession I truly care about—and headed for the back of the house. We don't have a back door—but at least I figured I could jump out the window.

*BOOM BA-BOOM BOOM.*

I got to the back window. My hands were shaking as I tried to open it. It was painted shut!

*BOOMBOOMBOOM.*

I was going to have to defend myself. I ran into the other room, dropped the guitar, the butcher knife clenched in my hand. Then a voice came through the door. "Chass! Hey, Chass! You in there?"

A wave of relief flooded through me. It wasn't a man's voice. It was just my crazy friend Katie. I threw open the front door.

Katie stood there in a parka, her eyebrows and hair full of snow, her skin pale from the frigid wind.

"Blue Foot in the house!" she shouted as she walked

in. Then she looked at me curiously. "What's up with the butcher knife, dude?"

I looked down at my hand. "Oh!" I said. "Long story."

She pushed past me into the house. "Man, it sucks out there!" she said. "Thank God you were here. I've been wandering around out there for like an hour. You can't see jack out there. Smart you for not going out."

"Oh, I was out there myself," I said. I paused. "There's . . . actually . . . Miss Hill? From school?"

"Pruneface?"

"Yeah. She's dead. Somebody murdered her across the street. I found her."

Katie was halfway out of her coat by then. She stopped taking the coat off. "What!" she said.

I nodded. "Shot. I think I saw the guy who did it."

She stared at me, frozen, halfway out of her coat. "Dude, you're joking."

I shook my head.

As the realization set in that I wasn't joking, a cascade of expressions passed over her face. Shock, then sadness, then a few others. But the one that finally stuck was excitement.

Katie did a movie-announcer voice: "They were trapped in the small snowbound town of Hickville,

Minnesota. One twisted psychopath. Two teenage girls. A terrible game of cat and mouse. Will our two heroines uncover the truth before they, too, fall victim to the sick, twisted, insane—"

"Dude!" I said.

"Wait!" Katie said. "I still haven't thought up a name for him. A terrible game of blah blah blah, where was I? Oh yeah: Will our two heroines reveal the truth before they, too, fall victim to the . . . uh . . . the Snow Killer. No no no, wait. The Hickville Sicko. Mr. Freeze. No, that's already been taken. Wait! Wait!"

"Dude," I said. "Look, I'm not trying to . . . It's just . . . I've been through this before. It's not funny."

Katie still had the coat half off. Suddenly she dissolved in tears. "She's really dead? Miss Pruneface? She's really, honest-to-God—"

"Yeah," I said. "She really is."

"Why?" she shouted. Tears were streaming down her face. "Everybody loved Miss Pruneface. She was a pain in the ass, but God, she was like the *best*!" Mascara was leaking all over her face. "The best!"

"Yeah," I said. "I know. I liked her, too."

"Crap," Katie said. "This really sucks. This isn't right."

"No," I said.

She went over to the window, peeped out at the blinding snow. "So whoever did it . . ."

"Uh-huh," I said. "He's still out there."

We stood there for a long time, not saying anything. Finally Katie went over and locked the door. "Why would somebody do something like that?"

I had the funniest feeling. I felt like I was on the edge of something. I wasn't sure what it was, exactly. For sixteen years now I'd been traveling around with my mother, changing names all the time, changing identities, never really having a chance to get close to much of anybody. My sort-of boyfriend Ben back in Alabama was probably as close as it got.

What I'd come to realize was that the closer I got to anybody, the more I had to lie. *Where are you from?* someone would ask. And then out would come a lie. *You ever been to the Grand Canyon? Ever been on an airplane? Did your old school have a debate club? What happened to your dad?* Lie, lie, lie, lie, lie.

Of course, like I was saying earlier, Mom doesn't call them lies. She calls it, The Legend. But what is The Legend if not just a big pile of lies?

Katie called herself my best friend. But the truth is, she didn't know me. She didn't know me at all. And whose fault was that? Not hers.

51

And then, without making a decision, I made a decision.

"Sit down," I said. "I have to tell you the truth."

She sat down, sniffling and wiping her face. "About what?"

"About . . . everything." I took a deep breath. I knew Mom would kill me if she knew what I was going to do. But I was sick to death of all this lie lie lie lie lie stuff. "My real name isn't Carla Darden. It's not even really Chass . . ."

And then I told her everything. I told her about what happened to my mom before I was born, about how Kyle Van Epps killed my father, about how Mom stole this tape that had Kyle Van Epps's confession on it, about how Kyle Van Epps had been trying to track us down and get that tape back. I told her about how he finally caught up to us in Alabama. I told her about some strange experiences I had a few months ago in San Francisco, where I managed to solve the murder of a famous pop star. And finally I stopped and said, "So that's it. Now you know who I really am—could you still be my friend?"

Katie was staring off into space. Finally, without a word, she stood up, put on her coat, walked to the door, and went out into the snow.

The door closed with a sharp thump. I sat down on the couch, put my face in my hands, and started to cry.

*I should have just lied!* I thought bitterly. Now I'd lost a friend *and* I'd let the cat out of the bag about who we really were.

After about a minute there was a soft knock on the door.

"What!" I shouted. I figured Katie was going to come back and tell me what a big hateful lying jerk I was.

The door opened a crack. Katie peeked in. "Um," she said. "I left my mittens."

She came in and put the mittens on. I looked at the floor. Then she took the mittens off again and dropped them on the floor. Then she took off her coat and dropped it on the floor, too.

"I'm sorry," I said. "I understand if you don't want to be friends with somebody who lies to you all the time."

She shook her head, sighed really loudly, and flopped down on the couch. "It's not that," she said. "It's the whole opposite."

I looked at her curiously.

"I'm a big fat liar, too," she said. She stared up at the ceiling for a long time. "Everybody thinks the Blue Foot doesn't give a crap. Everybody thinks I'm indestructible. Everybody thinks I'm this crazy weirdo with all these piercings who doesn't care what anybody thinks." She laughed bitterly. "What a frickin' lie. I'm scared all the time. I'm a total phony-ass fake. I really wish I could just, like, wear pink sweaters and be a cheerleader and dye my hair blond and have everybody think I was pretty. God! I mean . . . I even love Jayson Norquist." Jayson Norquist was the star of the football team, the Fighting Gobblers. He already had a scholarship offer from one of the Big Ten schools.

"Well, hey," I said. "Everybody feels that way. Even I feel that way."

Her eyes widened. "*You're* in love with Jayson Norquist?"

"Well . . . no." Actually I thought he was a bogus douche bag. "The other stuff, I mean."

She seemed strangely relieved. "But why? I mean, you're so . . . *cool*. And you play guitar. You sing like a frickin' angel. And you wear a black leather jacket! Me, I have *nothing*! Plus, God, I would cut my left arm off to have your boobs."

Katie was tall and graceful and—when you got past her Goth weirdo makeup and all the metal sticking out of her face—really pretty. But she was right about the boob thing. Jayson Norquist probably had bigger boobs than she did.

I started laughing. I don't know what was so funny exactly. But *something* was. Then Katie started laughing, too. We both laughed for a long time.

Then, finally, when we stopped, she did her big sad sigh again, and said, "Anyway . . . that wasn't what I was really talking about. What I really was talking about was that—"

And then there was a loud banging on the door. We looked at each other.

"Hey!" a man's voice called loudly. "Hey, Chass, I know you're in there! Give it up and open the door!"

"Oh, *snap*!" Katie whispered. Her face had gone white. "What are we gonna do?"

I started dragging the couch over toward the door. Katie jumped up to help. In a few seconds we had it jammed up against the front door. The man outside was still pounding away.

"Open up!" the man yelled. "You're never gonna get away from me, so you might as well open the door!"

"That's what they always say!" Katie said. "Next thing you know they're draping your guts across the bedposts."

"Thanks for that heartening image," I said. Then I ran back into the bathroom again. This time I had an idea. I jabbed the butcher knife I'd been carrying into the bottom of the window and jerked hard on it. I figured it would pry open the window. Instead, the blade snapped in half.

But as it snapped, I saw a thin black line open up in the paint that had sealed the window shut. I banged it with the palms of my hand and then pushed up. It came free.

"Hurry!" I hissed. "You first."

Katie blinked.

"Out the window. Now!"

It was a small window. Katie climbed on the toilet, wriggled out. I followed her. In the falling snow she looked ghostly, lying on the ground underneath the window. It was a long fall. For a moment I thought she might have injured herself badly.

Her eyes blinked open. "*Ow,* that hurt!" she whispered. Then she jumped up, a dark form in the gray swirling snow. I pushed through, dropped, landed on my back.

She was right. It hurt like a son of a gun! But the snow was thick enough that it cushioned my fall a little and I wasn't injured.

I stood unsteadily. I realized then that I'd made a big mistake. I'd forgotten to put my coat on. It was somewhere around twenty-five degrees, a whiteout snowstorm—and I didn't have my coat on. Great.

As I was trying to figure out what to do next, a dark figure swam out of the falling snow. "Don't move a muscle, Chass," he said, "or I swear to God I'll kill you."

I stared at him. The man standing over me was a tall black guy, so handsome he almost qualified as beautiful. Tattoos crawled up the sides of his neck, and his eyes were a strangely iridescent green.

"*Fabe?*" I said incredulously.

# SIX

**SO I GUESS** I have to back up a little. When I was out in California, I formed a band. Fabe Daniels was my drummer. He was not only a nice guy, he was the most ridiculously great drummer I've ever heard.

Mom and I had to leave California on pretty short notice. But as I was leaving, Fabe told me he was going to find me again. At the time I thought he was blowing smoke.

I guess I was wrong.

Fabe grinned at me. "Surprise!" he said.

"How in the world did you find me—"

"The Internet," he said. "How do you think? I used this fuzzy logic search tool that correlates—"

I cut him off. You wouldn't know it from looking at him, but Fabe's also a total geek. He can go on about stuff like that until your head about explodes.

"You almost gave me a heart attack!" I said, jumping up from the snow. I punched him in the chest. "I could have killed myself jumping out of that stupid window!"

I gave him a hug, then I turned to Katie.

"This is my friend Fabian Daniels," I said.

"Fabe," he said. "Only my mom calls me Fabian."

Katie gawked at him. There were not a lot of guys who looked like Fabe in Greenville, Minnesota. Actually, none.

"Let's get inside," I said. We trudged back around the building, back up the stairs, and into the apartment.

"Well, I guess this answers one question," I said as we sat down in the living room. "The mysterious guy from California didn't kill Miss Hill."

"Huh?" Fabe said.

"You caught me on a weird day," I said. "A lady

who teaches at our school got murdered just a little while ago."

"Man!" Fabe said. "That's awful."

I was happy for a chance to change the subject. Miss Hill's dead face kept popping into my mind . . . and I really wished it would go away. "So," I said. "Fabe, what are you doing here?"

He looked me in the eye. "I told you I was going to find you," he said.

"Wow, this so romantic!" Katie said.

Fabe laughed. "Nah, nothing like that. Chass is far too young for an old geezer like me." Fabe is like twenty-five. "I got a call from this guy who heard you last year. He runs a booking agency and wanted to book a tour for you this summer."

I wrinkled my forehead. "What do you mean?"

"A tour. That's a thing that musicians do where they travel around in a very small van, smelling each other's farts and—"

"I'm serious!"

Fabe laughed. "You did a couple of demos over at my studio, remember? One of them got to this manager guy. He thinks that on the strength of those demos and a couple of photos, he can get you thirty to forty gigs this summer. Serious gigs. Not coffeehouse, hundred-dollar-a-night dates. I'm talking real money, real venues, real gigs."

"But—"

"We wouldn't even have to do it under your name. There's no reason Kyle Van Epps would be able to find out about it. We'll just come up with a band name."

"That's crazy!" I said. "A *tour*? I'm sixteen."

"So? I'll make sure you don't get in any trouble. I'll straighten it out with your mom."

I shook my head. "Mom's gonna flip. Not so much about the touring thing . . . but because you came out here. She's gonna say somebody probably followed you. She's going to make us leave Greenville."

"No!" shouted Katie at me. "You can't *leave*! That's totally not allowed."

Fabe shook his head. "Nobody followed me. I didn't tell a single soul I was coming. I turned off my cell phone so nobody could track me electronically. I paid cash for everything. I haven't used a credit card. I watched my rearview mirror the whole way out here. There's no way anybody could have traced me out here. No way."

I scratched my head.

"So, Chass," Fabe said, grinning, "you want to go on tour or not?"

"What about—"

"Everybody's in. Marco, me, Annie—we're all in."

"So you told them you knew where I was?"

Fabe's smile faded. "I just said, 'Look, if I can find Chass, will you tour with us?' I didn't tell them where you were. I didn't even tell them I'd found you. I've been very, very careful."

I looked at Katie.

"Are you crazy, dude?" she said. "Your own national tour? You *have* to go!"

I shrugged, then laughed. "Well, hey, I guess I have no choice."

"The Blue Foot could be your roadie!" Katie said. "I'm totally in!"

Fabe smiled. "See? I knew if I drove all the way out here . . ." He stretched and yawned. "Oh, man, I'm tired. I drove for like twenty-four hours straight. I think it's finally catching up with me. I guess I better get back to my hotel."

"You can't drive out there," I said.

"Yeah, I found that out the hard way," he said. "I drove my car into a ditch a few minutes ago."

"Well, then why don't you lie down on the couch?"

"Hey, I don't want to get in your way."

"Look at you," I said. "You're not dressed for this

weather. You could get lost and freeze to death. Anyway, I won't even be here."

"Where are you going?" Katie said.

"I was so fixated on the man-from-California thing that I kind of forgot about something."

"What's that?" Katie said.

"I saw the guy who killed Miss Hill."

"So?"

"Well, if I saw him . . . then he saw me. He could be coming after me right this minute."

Katie's eyes widened. "Oh God! I hadn't even thought of that!" She frowned. "But you said you couldn't make out his face. Maybe he couldn't make out yours."

"I can't take that chance. He was wearing a hat and sunglasses and his collar was pulled up. I didn't even have a hat on. He probably saw me better than I saw him."

Katie swallowed.

"I've got to find out who he is," I said. "Before he finds me. Maybe we'll figure out where Mom is while we're at it."

"But . . . how?"

"Come with me," I said. "I have an idea."

# SEVEN

**KATIE AND I** left Fabe on the couch—where he had already fallen asleep—and headed out into the snow. The storm had slacked off a little. Not enough that you could drive . . . but enough that you could at least see across the street.

"Okay," I said as we walked out into the snow, "so the killer is not some hired assassin from California. It's somebody local."

"That makes sense."

"So who'd want to kill her? Who hates her?"

Katie looked thoughtful. "She's kind of crotchety. But I wouldn't say anybody *hates* her. Well, except Mr. Osmund."

Mr. Osmund was the principal of Greenville High. "Why does he hate her?"

"You know Mr. Osmund. He only likes brown-nosers. Miss Hill's like the opposite of a brownnoser."

"Huh," I said. "Interesting."

"They had some kind of big fight a few years ago. Supposedly they haven't spoken since. At school, they would pass in the hall and just walk right by each other." Katie rubbed her mittens together. "So . . . where are we going?"

"To Miss Hill's house," I said.

As I've said, Greenville is a very small town. Our music teacher's house was only a short walk from where we lived. Even with the snow halfway up to our knees, it still only took about fifteen minutes to walk there.

Miss Hill had lived in a one-story wood-frame house on Cove Street.

"Look!" Katie said.

I saw it, too. A set of barely visible depressions led up to the house. Footprints. There were no footprints coming out.

Katie's voice dropped to a whisper. "You think somebody's inside?"

"Let's check," I said.

"You're joking, right?"

I shook my head. My heart was racing. But I figured if the killer was in there, we could always run. Besides, honestly, I couldn't really tell if the footprints were going in or out. Maybe it was Miss Hill's footprints from when she left. I would have thought they'd have been covered up by now. But who knows?

Katie grabbed my arm as we walked to the front door. I knocked loudly. No answer.

"Nobody's there," Katie said, sounding relieved. "I guess we can go."

I noticed the snow started coming down even heavier. The houses across the street had disappeared again.

"We need to go in," I said.

Katie rubbed her hands together nervously. She looked up and down the street. Then she leaned toward me and whispered, "I've never told anybody this before—but I know how to pick locks."

"Before we get all cat burglar here . . ." I said. I put my hand on the knob and twisted. The door opened easily.

"Oh," Katie said. "Kinda didn't think of that."

I laughed softly, then eased the door open. "Anybody home?" I called. "Hello?"

I wasn't really expecting an answer. But I figured if the killer was there, maybe I'd scare them into running out the back door. I walked tentatively into the front room, peered around. I don't know what I'd expected. Something old-lady-ish, I guess? Overstuffed chairs with antimacassars and black-and-white pictures of long-dead family members, that sort of thing. Instead I found myself in a bright modern room. The walls were hung with pictures of jazz musicians. The furniture was white leather, like something out of an architecture magazine.

"What are we looking for?" Katie whispered.

"Clues," I said.

"Oh." She made a face. "Like, what kind of clues?"

"I have no idea," I whispered back.

"Why are we whispering?" she whispered.

"I have no idea," I whispered.

Suddenly we both burst out in loud, nervous laughter.

I slipped out of my heavy boots so I wouldn't drip mud all over the floor and began walking around in my socks. "I guess we need to be careful not to leave fingerprints or anything like that," I said. "We don't want to mess things up for the crime-scene people."

"I hadn't thought of that," Katie said.

Everything in the house was extraordinarily neat—a place for everything and everything in its place. I noticed a cordless phone lying on the kitchen table. That seemed uncharacteristic. Based on the way everything else in the house looked, I would have thought Miss Hill would have put the phone back in the charger. I got a paper towel from the kitchen, picked up the phone so that I wouldn't leave fingerprints.

I tried the number that Mom and I use for voice mail, but it didn't do anything.

Katie riffled through a stack of mail by the door, picked up a bill, and held it up. "Her phone company is Comcast," she said. "Star-nine-nine gets you voice mail."

I dialed *99. "You have no new messages," the voice said. "First saved message . . ." A man's voice came on. "I'm sick of this, you twisted old bat!" the man shouted. "I've given you every opportunity. And what do you do? Once again, you bite the hand that feeds you. You keep pushing and you're going to be sorry, sorry, *sorry*. That's all I have to say." Then there was a loud click, like someone on the other end had slammed down the phone.

I felt a shiver run down my spine. I knew that voice. It was Mr. Osmund, our principal.

"What?" Katie said.

I held the phone up to her ear and replayed the message.

"Whoa!" she said.

I set the phone down exactly where I'd found it and walked down the hallway to the back of the house. I was shocked at what I found. Unlike the neat living room and kitchen, Miss Hill's bedroom looked like a war zone.

"Holy crap!" Katie said, peering over my shoulder.

Pictures had been torn off the wall and smashed on the floor. The mattress had been pulled from the bed and the top layer cut open and peeled back so that all the springs were exposed. Clothes lay on the floor, drawers were spilled open, and the bedside table had been knocked over.

"Somebody was sure looking for *something*," Katie said.

"I wish we knew what they were looking for," I said.

I backed into the hallway, pushed open the next door. It was a small music studio full of beautiful state-of-the-art recording equipment. Well . . . it *had* been beautiful recording equipment once. Now it was broken junk, strewn all over the floor. Mixing boards, pre-amps, compressors—all kinds of recording gear, smashed. It made me want to cry.

"Who would do something like this?" I said.

Katie shook her head. I waded into the room, started picking things up at random. I'm no expert on home recording studios, but this stuff was seriously high-quality equipment. Fabe owned a really nice recording studio back in San Francisco, and I had spent enough time there to recognize good-quality gear.

"Don't move!" a man's voice said.

I whirled around. Standing in the doorway was Chief Norgren. He was pointing a long pistol at me and Katie.

I was holding a black metal box in my hand. No clue what it was . . . but it looked expensive. I let it drop back into the pile of wrecked equipment.

"Uh . . ." I said. "I can explain."

"I think maybe I've heard enough of your explanations for today," Chief Norgren said. "Now turn around and lace your fingers behind your heads."

Fifteen minutes later, Chief Norgren was herding us into the police station, his gun still drawn. Katie and I were handcuffed. Katie was sobbing.

"Look, it's not her fault," I said. "She was just following me."

"Not another word," Chief Norgren said, "until I've advised you of your rights."

"My *rights*!" I said. "We were just trying to—"

"You have the right to remain silent. Anything you say can and will be used against you in a court of law . . ."

He went through the whole rigmarole, made us both sign a piece of paper showing that we understood everything.

"How old are you girls?" Chief Norgren said.

"Seventeen," Katie said.

"Sixteen," I said.

"Crap," Chief Norgren said. "That means you're a minor, Chass. Where's your mom?"

"I don't know."

"I can't question you until she gets in here," he said.

"I don't need to be questioned!" I shouted. "If you'd stop treating us like criminals and listen to what we have to say—"

Chief Norgren stuck his fingers in his ears. "La-la-

la-la-la," he said. "I'm not listening. I'm not listening till your mom gets here."

I looked at Katie. I couldn't believe what I was seeing. We might have discovered some serious clues and here this clown was sticking his fingers in his ears and acting like a four-year-old.

Katie seemed less appalled than me. "I can't believe you got me into this, Chass!" she said. "Why did I go in there with you? Why did I listen to you?"

"If you'd take my handcuffs off, Chief," I shouted, "I could write down my mom's phone number and you could call her."

I guess Chief Norgren could hear me because he took his fingers out of his ears. "Okay, tell me her number."

I told him the number. I had to tell him three times because he kept getting confused. Finally he got it right. The more I saw of Chief Norgren, the less impressed I was. He listened to his phone for a minute then said, "Tell me again?"

I rolled my eyes, told him the number for the fourth time.

He dialed it again, then slammed the phone down on the desk. "Durn it!" he said. "Darn durn daggit!"

"What?" I said.

"Cell phone service is out." He covered his head with his hands and rubbed back and forth like he was trying to scrape all the hair off his head. I could see the poor guy was in over his head in a big way. "The cell-phone tower ices up every time we get a big storm and then the service goes out." He paced up and down. "Dadgum sheriff's department can't get here from Morris until the dadgum snowplows get out. The dadgum state patrol can't dadgum get through either, and the dadgum BCA's stuck in Brainerd. Dadgummit!" He picked up the phone and slammed it repeatedly on the desk. "Dadgummit*gummit*! Dadgummit all to gosh dang blam blame cockadoodiddley *dang* it!" He was literally jumping up and down now, his fists balled up, his knuckles white.

"Would it help you to just go ahead and say a bad word?" I said. "You could maybe warm up by trying *crap* and then move on to something a little stronger, like maybe—"

Chief Norgren turned and stared at me with about the angriest stare I've ever seen in my life. "You think this is some kind of *joke*?" he shouted.

"I'm just trying to—"

"I sat there listening to all your malarkey—and then you waltz off and break into her house and trash her things. For all I know, you're the one who killed that poor lady!"

"Hey," I shouted back. "If you would have just listened to me for like a second instead of jumping to conclusions—"

"Shut up!" We both looked over at Katie. She had her hands pressed over her ears. "Both of you shut up shut up shut up!"

For a minute nobody spoke. Chief Norgren's eyes had gone wide.

Finally Chief Norgren spoke: "Uh, hon, how did you get your hands out of them handcuffs?"

"Yeah," I said. "How *did* you?"

"I told you"—she sniffled—"I know how to pick locks."

Chief Norgren threw up his hands and stared at the ceiling. "What next?" he said. "I'm just one man, Lord. Murders I can handle. But teenage girls who pick the locks on their handcuffs?"

Katie wiped at her face, smearing her Goth mascara all over the place. She looked like a raccoon now. "We were just trying to help," Katie said softly.

Chief Norgren pulled some keys off his belt, unlocked my cuffs. "All right, all right, all right, all right," he said, blowing out a long breath. "Let's go back to square one. I'm just gonna take a chance here that you gals aren't murderers and throw all the rules of evidence out the window. Now look, what were you girls doing over there?"

Katie looked at me. I looked at Katie. Finally I spoke. "Here's the thing," I said. "The guy who shot Miss Hill—he saw me. He saw my face. Now, like you've said, there's no law enforcement in this town but you. No state patrol, no state police, no FBI, no nothing. No offense, Chief, but you've got a lot on your hands. So I'm pretty much on my own here. If that guy thinks I can ID him, he's going to come after *me*. And I've got nowhere to go. I can't leave town in this." I pointed out the window. The wind had picked up. It was howling out there now, the snow driving almost parallel to the ground. "So I figure, hey, I might as well go after him. Right? Get to him before he gets to me."

Chief Norgren scratched at his little mustache a couple of times. "Well, I guess I can't fault your logic. Your common sense, maybe. But not your logic."

"Anyway," I said, "we found a message on her phone. A threatening message. It was from Mr. Osmund."

"*Paul* Osmund? Your principal?"

We nodded. The wind had started causing a spooky

rattling noise from something in the roof of the police station.

"Oh, my word," he said. "I always knew that feud would get him in trouble."

"What's it about?" I said. "Their feud, I mean?"

Before he could answer, there was a strange howling groaning shriek from outside.

"What *is* that?" Katie said.

And then there was a humongous crash and the entire far wall of the police station collapsed.

For a moment no one moved. Chief Norgren had thrown himself on the floor, arms over his head. Katie and I were still sitting in our chairs, stiff as statues. After about five seconds, Chief Norgren's head popped up over the top of the desk. "I'm okay!" he said. "I'm okay!" Then, probably realizing how ridiculous he looked, he said, "You gals okay?"

We nodded.

Sticking through the ceiling in the caved-in part of the station was an ice-encrusted metal pole about two feet in diameter. Snow blew in through the walls and ceiling. "Well," Chief Norgren said, "I think we can count out using our cell phones for the duration."

It was the town's only cell-phone tower, a tall pole,

which, until this moment, had stuck up right in the middle of town.

Wordlessly we put on our coats, mittens, and hats. The frame of the front door was knocked out of whack, so Chief Norgren had to kick it open. We walked out into the street. For a moment the driving wind slackened. As it did so, visibility improved slightly. The top of the cell tower was visible. It had crashed down on top of the town's only police car, taken out a thicket of power lines and telephone wires, and was now blocking all of Broad Street.

Standing in the middle of the street was a gray shape, staring at us. A wolf.

For a moment the three of us stared at the wolf. Then, soundlessly, it leaped over the big steel pole and disappeared into the snow.

Chief Norgren pulled out his revolver, pointed it into the swirling gray emptiness, and fired until it started making a clicking noise.

I exchanged glances with Katie. I could see we were in agreement. This guy was losing it. We left Chief Norgren pacing in the snow, talking to himself and shaking his head.

# EIGHT

**"WHAT FEUD DO** you think he was talking about?" I said as we trudged through the blinding snow.

"Huh?" Katie said.

"Chief Norgren. When I told him about the message, he said something like 'I always knew that feud would get him in trouble.' What's it all about? Why did they not get along?"

"I don't know. It's just one of those things. They've always hated each other."

"But why?"

"You know who'd know?" Katie said. "Christie Dauntless."

Christie Dauntless was a girl in our school. She was one of those busybody-type people who knew everybody in the town and gossiped more or less constantly about all of them.

"And if she doesn't know," Katie added, "her mother will for sure."

"Where does she live?"

"Well, that's the problem. They're a good way outside town."

As we were talking, I heard an engine noise behind us. "Look out," I said. "I already about got run over once today."

And then there was something looming up over us. A truck. It stopped, and the door opened. "Ho! Coulda rode right over ya!" a voice called out. Then a figure emerged from the cab. I recognized him as a kid from school. I didn't really know him. He was a senior named Kenny Irvstedt, one of those farm-type guys who seems to be allergic to any clothes that aren't made from camouflage. I sometimes wondered if guys like him wore camouflage underpants.

Now that the truck was stopped, I could see it was

one of those jacked-up pickup trucks with huge knobby tires and all kinds of lights and roll bars and stuff.

"You gals need a ride?" he said. He had snuff under his lower lip. He spit a big blob of brown spit in the snow. "Kinda dangerous out here."

I looked at Katie and grinned.

"Hi, Kenny," she called. "You think you could get us out to Christie Dauntless's place?"

He whacked his truck on the hood with one hand. "If this truck can't get ya there, it ain't worth going to," he said. "Hop in."

We didn't have to be asked twice.

The inside of Kenny's truck was warm as Florida.

"Heard you found Miss Hill," he said to me. "Musta been a heck of a shock, huh?"

"How in the world did you find that out?" I said. "There's a whiteout snowstorm."

"I had noticed," he said. He was crawling along at about two miles an hour, not looking in any kind of rush. When I saw how slow he was going, I realized why I'd wrecked the snowmobile. The trick to driving in this weather was obviously to go about the speed that I run the mile in PE. Which, in case you were wondering, is SLOOOOOOOOWWWWWWWW.

"Poor old Miss Hill," the boy said. "You don't want

80

to point fingers or nothing . . . but boy, you gotta figure Chief Norgren's gonna take a darn hard look at Mr. Osmund, huh?"

"Could be," I said.

Kenny took a paper cup off the dash and spit into it. There was about an inch of disgusting tobacco spit in it. "Okay, Kenny," Katie said, "if that falls off the dash on me, I'm gonna get medieval on you."

"Sorry," Kenny said, reaching across me and putting it in the glove box. There were three more identical cups full of dried tobacco spit already sitting there, along with a bunch of Skoal cans.

"So . . ." I said. "Why do you think Chief Norgren should be suspicious of Mr. Osmund?"

"Look," he said, shutting the glove box, "I don't believe in gossiping."

"Sure," I said. "I understand."

He kept crawling along, the windshield wipers going at high speed, slinging snow off the windows by the handful.

"Of course, I forget," Kenny said to me after we'd gone four or five minutes in silence, "you're new around here."

"Yeah," I said.

"So you might not know about Miss Hill and Mr.

Osmund. They got a feud going. That's not gossip. I don't believe in gossip. Nah, see, that's just facts."

"I heard something about that," I said. "But what's it all about?"

"Pure hatred," he said.

"Mm," I said.

He drove some more.

"Originally, though?" He adjusted his cap—which, of course, was camouflaged and had the Buckmasters logo on it. "Originally, seems like I heard it had something to do with a student."

"How so?"

"Look, I'm one of these guys believes in getting up, doing my chores, go to school, help my dad in the fields, do a little hunting when I get a chance. Work hard, play fair, keep your mouth shut, ya know what I'm saying? No offense. Stay out of people's business."

"Sure," I said.

He made a whistling noise through his teeth. "Of course, hey, we're talking ancient history here. Back when they first started teaching at the high school—this must of been back in the sixties—Mr. Osmund and Miss Hill was teachers together. This was before Mr. Osmund became principal. They say Mr. Osmund had a thing for Miss Hill. Totally in love with her. But Miss Hill didn't care nothing for him. So then there was a story came out that Miss Hill was getting a little too familiar with a student, if ya know what I mean. Some people said Mr. Osmund was making things up. Some people said it was true. I couldn't tell you."

"Sure."

"I don't believe in saying a thing if it ain't fact," Kenny said.

"Sure."

"A man stands by his word. Say a thing if it's true. Otherwise, keep them lips closed." He made a zipping motion across his mouth.

"Sure."

He cleared his throat. "What I *will* say here— qualifying it to be a rumor which I don't know whether it's true or not—is that the summer after all these fingers was pointed, Miss Hill left town for the entire summer, didn't come back till the very first day of school. People that was there said she looked real pale and sickly. People asked her where she'd been, she told them she went to this here music college out in Colorado." Kenny adjusted his hat again. "But there was people wondering, how come ya go up there to the mountains, all that opportunity to get out in nature, etc. etc. etc., hiking, what have you?—how come ya come back looking so pale and funny? You see what I'm saying?"

"Um . . ." I said.

"Right!" Kenny said. "Exactly!"

I had no idea what he was talking about. "Spell it out for me," I said.

"I got no time for gossip," Kenny said.

"A man stands by his word," I said. "Say a thing if it's true. Keep to the facts."

Kenny nodded soberly. "That's what I'm saying. That's *exactly* what I'm saying." He fished around under his lip with his tongue, tamping down the wad of Skoal under his lip. "Sticking to facts completely, you got to ask what would cause a lady to be gone all that time, come back all sickly-looking. Letting the facts speak for themselves, you'd be liable to think, okay, pregnant."

"You would be liable to think that, wouldn't you?"

"You could hide it, see? Up till the end of school? Loose dresses, whatnot? Then you go off, have the baby, come back home, nobody's the wiser." Kenny looked over at me, raised one eyebrow. "I'd be less than honest if I said there was proof. Nobody never claimed there was proof. But if a student was to get a teacher, uh, in a family way, huh?—well, that's how it'd be handled. Back then, I'm talking about. Right?"

"I see exactly what you mean."

"Now, I suppose if the student which was involved, allegedly, which was *allegedly* involved, if he had spoke on the matter—or if Miss Hill had?—hey, we'd have the facts right there in front of us, wouldn't be no debate on the matter."

"Mm-hm."

"Me, I can't stand gossip. All these girls—no offense!—all these girls, yip yip yip yip yip yip, all day long talking about other people's business. I'm just a simple country dude, do what you do, don't talk about it. That's my philosophy." He pointed at the glove box. "You mind handing me—"

I opened the glove box, handed him his cup of spit. He dribbled brown juice into it, handed it back.

"Sorry about that," he said. "I know it's a gross and disgusting habit. I was planning on quitting soon as wrestling season was over, but I just can't seem to shake it."

I put the spit cup delicately back in the glove box. I was like a brain surgeon—*that* careful. No way was I gonna drip that junk on my leg or something!

"Sticking to facts and facts alone, though, you'd be

moved to ask if there *was* a baby, well, what happened to it? Correct?"

"Correctamundo," Katie said. There was just a tiny, teeny bit of sarcasm in her voice.

"What?" Kenny said, giving her a hard look. He seemed insulted by something in Katie's tone of voice. "Did I say something funny?"

"No, no! Go on!"

"Yeah," I said. "I like how you just stick to the facts."

"You got *that* right," he said, still glaring at Katie. "Here I am doing ya a favor and everything."

"Absolutely," I said. "Absolutely."

Kenny stuck his chin out and kept his eyes glued to the road. It was no joke trying to find your way through this weather. I had no idea how he was doing it. It seemed like magic to me that he was able to avoid running into anything. Much less actually getting us where we were going. But I guess he'd lived here a lot longer than me.

"So anyway," I said, "what happened between Miss Hill and Mr. Osmund?"

"Not entirely clear," Kenny said. "Everybody knows they don't like each other. Over the years they've fought over all kind of stuff at school. What classes she gets to teach, how much money the pep band gets—all kind of boring stuff that nobody else cares about."

"So that's it?"

Kenny cleared his throat. "Well . . . they *say*—and, look, I'm just telling you what the word around town is and not nothing I seen with my own eyes—but they *say* that Miss Hill receives money from the kid she might or might not have had that baby with back in the sixties. Which, of course, he ain't a kid anymore. I guess he'd be a fairly old dude by now."

Kenny pushed in the clutch and let the truck coast to a stop.

"Regular money from that fellow. Regular as clockwork."

"Interesting," I said.

"Here we are," he said.

I looked out the window. All I could see was a blur of gray confetti.

"So what did you need to talk to Christie about in the middle of a snowstorm like this?"

Katie and I looked at each other.

"Now that I think about it?" I said.

"Pretty much nothing," Katie said.

"Yeah," I said. "Pretty much nothing at all."

Kenny shook his head once, like he was perplexed

by the mysteriousness of women. But he didn't say a word. Then he turned around and started crawling back through the snow.

"You know," he said after about five minutes, "bringing up them two reminds me of a funny story I heard the other day. This ain't gossip. I'm just relating the plain facts..."

We rumbled along through the snow while Kenny gossiped about probably everybody who'd ever lived in the entire city of Greenville.

Finally, when we got back to town, he stopped and we got ready to get out.

"Oh, hey," I said. "Something just struck me. The student. The one who might have gotten Miss Hill pregnant. What happened to him? Does he still live here?"

"That's why we won't never know the truth," Kenny said. "He moved away."

"Oh yeah?"

"Yeah, he left town, never came back. Most successful individual ever to have lived in Greenville. He sends money back for all kind of things. He donated the money for the baseball fields over on the other side of the river. The Shetland and Pinto fields, not the Mustang Field, which was already built a long time ago."

"But he never comes back."

"Not never." He reached across the front seat and grabbed the door handle. "You might have heard of him, being you're a musician and everything."

"Oh, why's that?"

"He owns that big company." He looked at Katie for help. "What's it called?"

Katie shook her head. "No clue."

I don't know what it was, but I felt a tickle in the back of my head. "The student," I said. "What was his name?"

"Yeah, his family, of course, after the tragedy, they all moved away."

"Tragedy?" I said, the hairs suddenly sticking up on my neck.

"*Big* tragedy," he said. "Yeah. Big, *big* tragedy."

"You didn't say his name."

"I didn't, did I?"

"What was his name?"

He squinched up his face, thinking. "Fellow by the name of . . . lemme think now. Van Epps? Kyle, I believe it was. Kyle Van Epps."

Kenny slammed the door shut.

"Wait!" I shouted. "What was the big tragedy?"

But it was too late, the big truck had disappeared into the blinding snow.

# NINE

**I FOUND MOM** standing in the middle of the apartment, trembling, brandishing a large wooden salad spoon as though it were a billy club. She had heard the door open and whirled around. When she saw it was just me, she waved the salad spoon at Fabe, who was sitting on the couch looking nervous.

"What is *he* doing here?" she shouted.

"Where have you been?" I shouted back. "You scared the crap out of me."

"The power went out. I went downstairs to see if they had any power down at the snowmobile dealership, and then I got stuck listening to Mr. Krieghoff go on a big tirade about how you'd stolen his—"

"Borrowed," I said. *"Borrowed."*

"Whatever," Mom said. "Not important. The important thing is that Fabe has probably just led Van Epps's people right *to* us!"

Her voice was high and piercing. Mom had been a professional singer a long time ago, so when she felt like shouting, she could about bust your eardrums.

"He says he was careful," I said softly. "And I believe him."

She looked at Fabe, then back at me. "What?" she said finally. "What are you looking at me like that for?"

*"He's* endangering us?" I said.

Mom looked at me blankly.

*"He's* the problem?"

"What!" Mom said. "Just spit it out, whatever it is that's—"

"When were you planning on telling me that Kyle Van Epps grew up here? Huh?"

Mom's face fell. She looked at the floor.

"I mean, we're supposed to choose where we go at

random! That's supposed to be what keeps us safe. We don't go anyplace he might expect us."

Mom sighed loudly. "Look, he hasn't stepped foot in this town for forty years. We have nothing to worry about."

"Then why are we here? Either there's something important here—in which case he might be keeping an eye on the town—or there's not—in which case, why bother coming here?"

"It's not that simple," Mom said.

"All you had to do was tell me!" I said.

"Could we not do this in front of the peanut gallery?" Mom said, waving her hand at Fabe and Katie.

"They already know," I said.

Mom blinked. "Both of them? You've told both of them about us?" Her face hardened. "Who have you *not* told?"

"Uh . . ." Katie said, "you know what? Maybe I should just go."

"Me, too," Fabe said.

"No!" I said. "You're not going anywhere. You're gonna sit right down while Mom explains in detail what the hell we're doing in Greenville, Minnesota!"

"Watch your mouth, young lady!" Mom said.

"Hey, hey, hey," Fabe said softly. "Look, maybe we should all take a thirty-second break, huh?"

Mom and I both glared at him.

"Or . . . not," he said, shrugging.

Mom and I caught each other's eyes. She probably saw the same thing in my eyes that I saw in hers: she looked a little embarrassed. We both struggled to stifle sheepish smiles. Fabe was right. Yelling at each other was not helping the situation.

Mom flopped onto the couch, gave Fabe a one-armed hug. "Not that I'm not glad to see you, Fabe . . ." she said.

"Hey, good to see you, too," he said.

Mom and Fabe had always liked each other. Once you got past the scary tattoos and the dreadlocks and the piercings, you saw that Fabe was an extremely polite, disciplined, serious guy. There was a calming steadiness about him that Mom appreciated.

Mom shifted around uncomfortably in the chair a couple of times. Finally she said, "Okay, so there are a few things I might have . . . neglected to tell you."

"All you had to do was say we were coming here to find out some stuff about Kyle Van Epps. Then I would have known."

"I guess I've just gotten in the habit of holding everything back from you. No matter what you think, you're still just a girl. I don't want you to feel like coming to this place is some kind of secret-agent assignment. I just want you to be a kid."

"Thanks," I said drily. "When the guy who blew Miss Hill away comes after me, I'll tell him to leave me alone because I'm busy just being a kid."

"Hey, it's easy to criticize." Mom's lip quivered a little. "I'm the mother. Sometimes, as a parent, you have to make hard decisions."

"Okay okay okay," I said. "Whatever. Please don't cry and make me feel like the ungrateful daughter. We're here now. So why don't you tell me what you expect to find."

She sighed heavily. "If we're ever going to get free of Van Epps," she said, "we have to start here."

"Why? What's here that's not anyplace else?"

"I don't know exactly. I just know that it started here."

*"It?"*

"I don't know exactly. I've been trying to find out everything I could about this guy for a long time. And the more I find out, the more I feel like there's something I'm missing. Something we could use to take him down for good."

"Like what?"

"Listen," she said. Then she stood up and walked over to our little boom-box CD player. She pulled a CD out of a drawer and slid it into the player. "Listen to this."

The stereo blasted out a rinky-dink song that sounded like it had been recorded several decades ago. The chorus went:

> *This is my confession*
> *Can't you see.*
> *If you want to find the real me*
> *I'll show you the key.*
> *It's buried where I lay my head*
> *Beside the willow tree.*

The singer's voice was great—strong, smoky, and kind of haunting—but the song seemed pretty lame. "Who's that?" I said.

"It's Kyle Van Epps."

"I didn't know he was a singer!" I said.

"Yep. He left Greenville when he was sixteen. He went to New York and recorded a couple songs. He had one hit called 'Why Should I Lie?' I actually found an old forty-five-rpm single of it." She pulled an old record in a crumbly paper sleeve out of the drawer and handed it to me. It listed the song on the record with the name of the songwriter underneath, *C. Van Epps*. I wondered why it was *C.* instead of *K.* Van Epps. I guess they didn't proofread it real carefully before they printed it. I slipped it back in the sleeve and handed it back to Mom.

"It went to Number sixteen, right between 'We'll Sing in the Sunshine' by Gale Garnett and 'It Hurts to Be in Love' by Gene Pitney. The song you're hearing was the B side, the other side of the single, the side of the record that nobody ever listened to. Anyway, Kyle started producing records for Apex Records soon after he recorded this song. By the time he was in his early twenties, he owned the company. The rest is history."

"And what about this song?" I said. "What's the big deal?"

"It's a code. I think he left something in this town, some kind of clue about himself. Something we can use to free ourselves from him."

"You mean you think there's something like . . . *literally* buried under a willow tree?" I said.

"Well, no. Under his bed, actually. 'Buried where I lay my head'—see? I found out where he used to live.

There's an old weeping willow right next to it! The house was abandoned. It collapsed a long time ago."

"Well, why haven't you gone up there and dug up the floor?"

"I have. I've gone over it with a metal detector. I've dug holes all over. And I've found nothing."

"So maybe it's not a clue after all," I said. "Or maybe he came back and dug it up later. Or—"

"Maybe," Mom said.

"Okay," Katie said, "what I don't get is why he would do it in the first place. Why leave a clue that could get him in trouble?"

Mom raised one eyebrow. "Because he's that kind of guy. He's the kind of monster who would think it was funny to leave a clue like that. To him, life is a big game."

"Hm," I said.

"Look, I can see you're skeptical," Mom said. "But think about it—why else would he have written a song like that in the first place? It's just so blatant. 'My Confession'? I mean, everything in the song refers to an event that happened here."

"What event?" I wondered if she was talking about the "tragedy" that Kenny Irvstedt had referred to.

Mom held up one finger. "I'll show you," she said.

"I was at the library the other day photocopying things from old newspapers. You can read them for yourself. They're down in the car."

She stood and pulled on her coat.

"It's pretty nasty out there," I said. "Why don't you just tell me."

"I meant to get them out of the car anyway," she said. She looked around like she'd left something somewhere. "I can't find my hat. Can I borrow yours?"

"It's right there," I said.

She pulled on my crazy hat, the bright yellow one with all the yarn hanging off of it.

"Back in a flash," she said. Then she barreled out the door.

"Do you know what Kenny Irvstedt was talking about?" I said. "Some kind of tragedy that happened to Kyle Van Epps's family?"

Katie shook her head. "I'm not much on town history," she said.

"You want some hot chocolate or something?" I said.

"That would be *great*," she said.

"Me too!" Fabe said.

We went into the kitchen and I started catching up with Fabe about what had been going on out in San Francisco since I left. I like to make hot chocolate the old-fashioned way, boiling the milk and stirring in the cocoa and the sugar. It takes longer, but it just tastes better than all that microwave junk.

I'd served up the cocoa, piled on a few marshmallows, and we were all sitting around sipping away when Katie said, "Where's your mom? Seems like it's taking an awful long time for her to get to the car and back."

"You think we ought to go out and look for her?" Fabe said after a few moments of silence.

Before I could answer, there was a loud thump on the door. Then nothing. I exchanged a nervous glance with Katie. Then I ran over and opened the door.

Mom was standing there in the snow with an odd grimace on her face. My goofy yellow hat was caked with ice, like she'd been lying in the snow.

"Mom?" I said. "You okay?"

She walked unsteadily into the room and started taking her coat off. Then her legs buckled and she fell to the floor.

"Mom!" I shouted.

As she hit the ground, her coat flapped open. I could see there was blood all over her chest.

"What happened, Mom?"

She gave me an odd apologetic smile. "I think . . . it looks like . . . I guess I kinda got shot."

# TEN

**THE POPULATION OF** Greenville is just under two thousand people. It's more than a wide spot in the road. But not by much. It has no hospital, no medical clinic. There's only one doctor. And from what I've heard, the doctor here spends a lot more time hunting and fishing than treating patients.

Still . . .

I grabbed the phone to call the doctor. There was

no dial tone. It was only then that I realized what had happened. When the cell tower fell, it had knocked down the phone lines, too.

"Phone's dead," I said. I knew Katie didn't have a cell phone. "Fabe? I don't suppose your cell is working?"

Fabe pulled his out, hit a button, then shook his head. "Nope. No signal."

I grabbed Mom's hand. "I'll be fine," she said. "It's just a flesh wound. Ha-ha."

But it wasn't funny. I could see she'd lost an awful lot of blood. Her face was white and her lips were pale.

"Where does the doctor live?" I said.

Katie looked out the window. "Two streets over."

"She can't go by herself," Fabe said. "Whoever shot your mom is still out there."

"Who did it, Mom?" I said.

Mom's lips moved. But then her eyes rolled back in her head and she slumped back down.

I felt this horrible sick sensation. "What's happening?" I shouted. "Mom! Mom, wake up!" I looked over at Fabe. "Fabe, help!"

"Get her feet up on that coffee table," he said. "She's not dying yet. It's shock. You just need to get her blood pressure up."

"How?"

"Just . . . put pressure on the wound!" he said, yanking on his jacket. "Keep her feet up!"

Katie was already heading out of the door. "Go!" I shouted.

The door slammed. They were gone. I did like he said. I got her feet up on the coffee table, then I put pressure on the wound."

"Ow!" Mom said, her eyes opening. "Jeee*sus,* that hurts!"

"Oh, thank God!" I said. I could feel tears practically exploding out of my eyes. "Thank God!"

I hugged Mom and sobbed on her chest.

"What happened?" she whispered vaguely.

"You were shot."

"Shot?" she said, staring at me. Then after a minute, she added. "Oh. Yeah. I remember now. Sort of." Then she sat up a little and looked around nervously. "You've got to go. Before he comes back."

"Who?"

She sucked in her breath raggedly. "I'm—I'm okay," she said. "I really don't think it hit anything vital." She pulled back the neck of her shirt and stared at the small, bleeding hole just below her collarbone. "Oh!"

she murmured. "Shouldn't have done that. Some things are better left—"

Then her mouth went slack and she fainted again.

"Mom!" The panic was running through me again. "Mom, please! Mom! Mom!"

In the movies when people get shot, everybody's always standing around saying snappy stuff. But in real life you just repeat the same words over and over.

After a minute Mom looked up at me, blinked, and said, "What happened? Why am I lying here?"

"You got shot," I said. "Remember? I already told you."

She looked at me blankly. "Oh. Yeah. Sorry."

Then she put her hand to the wound and winced.

"It'll be okay," I said. "Fabe and Katie went to get the doctor."

She shook her head. "You have to stop worrying about me. He's still out there."

"Who, Mom?" I said. "Who did this to you?"

"You have to go," she said. She was breathing hard, like she'd been running a race. "My pistol's . . . in my purse. Give it . . . to me. Lock the door. Then jump. Out the back . . . window."

"But the doctor won't be able to get in!" I said.

"Don't worry about that. Go!"

I dumped her purse on the floor. Mom has carried a pistol with her everyplace she's gone for as long as I've known her. It's a .38-caliber Smith & Wesson Airweight, if that means anything to you. The pistol spilled out on the cheap carpet. I put it in her hand.

"Thanks, honey," she said.

I gave her a hug, grabbed my coat, then ran into the bathroom and—for the second time of the day—crawled out the window and fell into the snow.

It wasn't until I hit the ground that I realized I still didn't know who shot her.

And maybe more importantly, I had no idea what to do next.

I stood up slowly, my glove pressed against the wall. If anything, the snow was coming down even harder than it had been earlier. I felt like I was in some science-fiction movie, standing next to a wall that disappeared into space. Like the entire universe had collapsed down to me, a ten-foot section of wall, and the falling snow. I shivered. If there was someone out there who wanted to kill Mom, they probably wouldn't mind knocking me off, too.

Where should I go? What should I do? I took a couple of breaths, feeling the sharp stab of the cold air deep in my lungs. It helped calm me down so I could think.

Whoever killed Miss Hill had probably shot Mom. Whoever shot Mom was probably connected to Kyle Van Epps. So Miss Hill's killer was probably connected to Kyle Van Epps, too. Once again, everything in my life was coming back to Kyle Van Epps.

I needed to find out more about him—where he'd lived, who he'd known, what he'd done in the few years he'd lived in Greenville.

I wished Katie was with me. She'd know who I should talk to. Failing that, who would know about Miss Hill?

Mr. Osmund, that's who. If you believed he had done it, then it seemed like a crazy place to start. He might try to kill me on the spot, right? But if Mr. Osmund *hadn't* killed Miss Hill—and I just couldn't believe that he had—then he might be able to point me in the right direction. And even if it *was* him, what was he going to do, blow me away in his living room, where I'd bleed all my DNA all over his carpet? No, I didn't think so.

Mr. Osmund lived about three blocks away.

I started walking. It took me a while, but eventually I found the house where Mr. Osmund lived. At least I was pretty sure that was it. To the degree that I could even see them, all the houses looked pretty much the same—like big snowy gray lumps with dim lights shining out here and there.

I trudged through the snowy yard and knocked on the door. A stocky elderly lady with very clear blue eyes and an unfashionable pile of hair answered. She was leaning on a cane. "Yes?" she said.

"I'm looking for Mr. Osmund," I said. "Is this the right house?"

"Mr. Osmund the principal or Mr. Osmund the plumber?"

"The principal."

The old lady frowned. "No, dear, he lives over on South Whitlock."

"I thought this *was* South Whitlock."

"This is North Myrtle."

I looked back in the direction of the last street sign I'd seen. I could have sworn it said East Whitlock. But maybe it had said *West* Whitlock. In which case I was in entirely the wrong part of town.

"It's just not safe to be out right now," the old woman said. She had a broad, somewhat ugly face, a strong jaw, and the sort of loud, insistent voice that people obeyed without question. Actually, she reminded me a little of Miss Hill in that respect. "Come inside immediately. You'll have a nice cup of hot chocolate while the snow calms down."

"Oh no," I said. "I really can't."

"Don't be stupid," the old woman said. Her face was stony. "It's not safe."

I really wanted to keep going. But East Whitlock was a pretty good distance from North Myrtle. A little bit of cocoa definitely wouldn't hurt. "Do you think maybe I could look at a map?" I said.

"See? Now you're thinking straight." She waved me into the house.

"Thank you."

She waved her hand dismissively. "You're the new girl," she said. It wasn't a question. "Carla Something. Durden? Darden?"

"Darden, yes, ma'am," I said. "But actually I go by Chass."

The old woman made a face of disapproval—though what it was she disapproved of, I couldn't tell.

"Sit," she commanded, pointing at a heavy old couch with her cane. I sat on the couch. "I'll be back with the map and the cocoa," she said.

I looked around the room. This was exactly the kind of house I would have thought Miss Hill would have lived in, but didn't. The furniture looked like it was all a hundred years old. There were black-and-white family photographs on the walls and a couple of paintings with religious themes. The house had a funny smell that I associate with old people. Not unpleasant—but distinctive. Musty air, mothballs, potpourri, that sort of thing.

"Well!" she said, placing an ornate china cup in front of me. "I should have introduced myself. I'm Mrs. Krauthammer. Mr. Krauthammer and I both joined the army and went to Europe. I was a nurse. I served in the Fifty-seventh Field Hospital in Prestwick, Scotland. Mr. Krauthammer, sadly, didn't make it back from the war. Survived D-day, then died in a jeep wreck in Paris. Ironic." She poured some hot chocolate into my cup, then poured some for herself. Then she poured about half an inch of whiskey in her own cup. "Medicinal purposes," she said.

I nodded soberly.

"That's a joke," she said, frowning at me. "You're permitted to crack a smile."

"Oh," I said. "Sorry. You never know around here. It's kind of a straitlaced town."

"It is," Mrs. Krauthammer said. She lifted her high-octane cocoa, took a long sip, set the cup back down. "So. You found Miss Hill."

"It only happened about two hours ago," I said. "Now everybody in town seems to know."

"Did you see who did it?"

I shook my head.

"You suspect it was Paul Osmund, though. So you're playing junior detective."

"Well . . ."

Mrs. Krauthammer was obviously one of those people who didn't converse. She lectured. "I don't think it was Paul Osmund," she said. "He's too weak. That's why he didn't like Miss Hill. She was stronger than he was, and she didn't mind letting him know. Men of his sort don't do well with that. I should know. Thirty years in the medical field. I never met a male doctor who didn't think he was smarter than I was. And they were generally wrong."

I took a sip of cocoa. It burned the crap out of my tongue. I don't know why, but every time I drink hot chocolate I burn my mouth. *Every* time.

"No," Mrs. Krauthammer said. "If I were a betting woman—which I am not—I would bet that it was your mother who killed Miss Hill."

"What are you talking about?" I said angrily.

Mrs. Krauthammer seemed not to be bothered by my outburst. "No, there's something about your mother that's not on the level. She's young. She's beautiful. She appears to be educated. She moves to a jerkwater little town in Minnesota where she knows no one. And she gets a job as a waitress. Doesn't add up."

"Now wait a minute—"

The old lady plowed on. "I'm a blunt woman, and I make no apologies for it. It's how God made me. I spoke to your mother once and asked her point-blank what she was doing here. She gave me an answer so cockamamie as to beggar belief."

What could I even say? Everything she said was true.

"And then to add to it, within ten minutes of her arrival in Greenville, your mother begins asking questions about a boy who left town forty years ago—a boy whose life was very much tied to that of Miss Hill."

"No," I said.

The old woman cocked her head and looked at me curiously. "No? No, *what*?"

"No," I said. "My mom didn't kill her. She was with me all morning. In fact, whoever killed Miss Hill, just shot my mom. My mom happens to be lying on the couch in our apartment, bleeding all over the place, hoping that the only doctor in this town can come and save her life. So if it's not too much trouble, could you stop saying nasty things about her?"

For the first time Mrs. Krauthammer smiled. It was a broad, bright smile, full of large crooked teeth. Her entire face lit up. "Well!" she said. "I like that. A girl with pep. Bravo!"

"Okay, so, yeah, you're right about one thing—we are here to find out about Kyle Van Epps," I said. Hey, I figured we'd be gone the second the snow stopped falling. So why worry about telling her? "He did something really bad to my mom. And Mom's been traveling around the country trying to find out about him so she can send him to jail."

Mrs. Krauthammer seemed just the tiniest bit taken aback. But then she rallied and the mask of indomitability dropped over her face again. "Well, then. You've come to the right place," she said. "I happen to know just about everything about just about everybody in this town. It's my . . . hobby."

"So you're the town busybody."

"I like to think of myself as the town historian." Her eyes narrowed with humor. "But it's a fine line, isn't it?" She clapped her hands together. "So. What do you need to know?"

"You said there was some kind of connection between Miss Hill and—"

She cut me off. "The Van Eppses." The old lady narrowed her eyes thoughtfully. "That's a rather tragic story."

"How so?"

"She was his second wife. Opal Van Epps, I'm talking about. Old Man Van Epps, Karl his name was, he was a good thirty years older than her. His first wife died. She was like a packhorse. Miserable creature. Never talked, never complained, just worked. Some people said she never had a thought in her mind. Just did what she was told. But that's what Karl wanted in a wife."

"What about—"

Mrs. Krauthammer looked irritated. "I'm getting there. Everybody today's in such a hurry. Why is that?"

I looked at my watch. I was wondering how Mom was doing. "I don't know, ma'am."

The old lady took a sip of her cocoa. "Karl Van Epps was a bad man. You know, there are men that are bad in a show-off way. Wrecking cars, getting sent to prison, putting tattoos on parts of their body that are meant to be hidden from the world. Not Karl. Maybe what made Karl worse, he didn't show off how bad he was. You had to get to know him a little just to see how evil he was."

"What did he do?"

Mrs. Krauthammer said, "When he was a boy, he pinned Emil Jenks to the ground and made him eat a handful of flies he'd grown off a dog turd in a jelly jar. He beat his own dog to death once. He secretly chopped down a man's apple tree once because the man had spoken to Karl's wife in a way that he considered to be overly familiar. Everyone knew he did it, but he never admitted to it. That was the kind of man he was, holding grudges, making nasty little plans, then doing things in secret to hurt you." She raised her eyebrows and looked out the window. "But it wasn't till after it happened that we knew the real depth of it. It wasn't till after, that we found out how bad it really ran."

"Until after what happened?"

Mrs. Krauthammer seemed not to notice me now, though. Her mind was someplace else.

"Poor Kyle. Poor, poor little Kyle—living in a house with a man like that."

I opened my mouth to ask another question. But then I realized that it was a waste of time. The old lady would tell the story of Kyle Van Epps. But it would come in its own way and in its own time. I just had to try my best to be patient.

"Karl's first wife hadn't been in the ground more than two or three weeks when he drove off in his pickup truck. He was gone about a week. He came back with a little girl next to him. When I say girl, I mean it. She looked like she was about sixteen years old. Come to find out later, she was only fourteen. Nobody knew, though. Nobody knew. That was Opal, the girl was.

"Later of course, we found out a great deal. But at the time all we knew was that Karl had driven up to Hemming, bought the girl from an old farmer and his wife up there. Bought her like livestock. They didn't mean anything by it. She was their granddaughter. They were ignorant stupid people, straight from the old country—Hungary, Albania, someplace like that—barely spoke English. That's how it was done back where they came from. A man comes, offers you a dowry for a girl, you take their money. They meant no harm to the girl. But of course, they could have looked at Karl and seen he was a bad man. But they didn't bother. They took the cash.

"So anyway, Karl took the girl around the town, introduced her. What he said, by way of direct quote was, 'What Mrs. Van Epps says has got my word behind it.' He wasn't trying to make his wife fit into the town or anything. He was just showing her off like you'd show off a new car. Now, she may have only been fourteen—but she was a woman all right. The most beautiful, exotic-looking creature you ever saw. And you could see she was a high-spirited one, too. As he took her around the town, she talked to the men, laughing and smiling right at them, Karl standing right there. And Karl didn't like it. I remember seeing it. I was standing in the back of the doctor's office. Karl introduced her to Dr. Newell. Now, Dr. Newell, he had an eye for the ladies. He or the girl—I couldn't tell you which one it was, but it was one of them—they made a joke. And Opal, she threw back her head and laughed. I could see the veins pulsing in her throat. She and Dr. Newell both laughed and laughed. But not Karl. I watched him watch her. There was a darkness on his face. And in that moment I had a terrible feeling. I had a feeling something bad was coming on. But I didn't know what.

"After that, we didn't see Opal for a long, long time. It must have been three, four years. When she finally come back to town, she was different." Mrs. Krauthammer looked thoughtful. "If anything, she was even more beautiful. But she was drawn out somehow.

There'd been a joy in her that first time when Karl brought her around the town. But now it was gone. She looked at the ground when she talked. If one tried to make a joke, she just looked away. Even if Karl wasn't standing there looking at her, she acted like he was, as though his eyes were pressing down on her all the time."

Mrs. Krauthammer refilled our cups with cocoa. This time she didn't add any whiskey to her own.

"Opal Van Epps was pregnant then. Pregnant with Kyle. After Kyle was born, Karl used to carry him into town, show him around. That was the closest that man ever got to seeming happy. When the boy was a baby, he'd show him off, squeeze his little arms, and say how strong he was, how he was going to make a good farmer someday.

"Now, Karl, bad man though he may have been, he was a superb farmer. Over time he bought up more land, more silos, more barns, more equipment. Eventually he had to hire a couple fellows to oversee the farm for him. Owned close to a square mile of property. It made him about the richest man in the county, other than old Doyle Redmun. But all that money didn't change him. He still lived in the same miserable old farmhouse he was born in, still drove the same old pickup truck from before the war.

"Karl's house was right on the edge of his land, not more than a stone's throw from the Heglunds—Millie and Dan. Millie and Dan Heglund, they used to talk around town, tell stories about sounds they heard coming from the Van Epps land. Said they heard moaning and wailing, things of that nature. Now, nobody gave them any credit. Millie and Dan were silly people. Dan wasn't much of a farmer and Millie never had a lick of sense. It was generally presumed that they were making all these stories up.

"Then one day Dan turned up dead, shot. It looked like a hunting accident. Karl come into town, told Chief O'Donnell that Dan was poaching deer on Karl's land, leaned his rifle on the fence between their properties, the gun somehow went off and killed him. Chief O'Donnell said the whole thing looked funny to him. But he couldn't prove anything.

"After that, though, Millie never said a word about strange sounds coming from Karl Van Epps's property. A couple of years later she sold the farm to Karl and moved down to the Cities to be with her daughter—the fat one not the pretty one.

"Meanwhile, little Kyle was growing up. He was the smartest boy in his class, the best athlete, the most popular, the most talented. He could sing, he could play the

piano, the harmonica, the trombone. He was a wres-
tler, too. He went undefeated till the state tournament
his sophomore year. Lost in the semifinals, I believe it
was, to a boy who went on to wrestle All-American at
U of Iowa."

I was getting nervous. The story was winding all
over the place, seemingly going nowhere. How long was
Mrs. Krauthammer going to go on? Was she ever going
to get to the point?

"Kyle!" the old woman said. "My goodness, what a
pretty boy he was. Every girl in Greenville loved him.
And every boy envied him." She shook her head sadly.
"I guess they wouldn't have if they'd known the truth.
If they'd known what was hidden back in that old farm-
house."

The room was very silent for a long time.

"What?" I said. "What *was* happening in the farmhouse?"

"He had a brother. That was what none of us knew.
Kyle had an older brother. He'd been born on the farm
out there sometime around 1947, 1948. A deformed
child. He wasn't crazy or a lunatic or retarded. But he
had this twisted back and this one little arm the size of
a doll's arm. And Karl didn't want anything that was
like that attached to his name. So he put the child in

the silo, figured he'd die out there. But the corn rotting out there gave off enough heat that the child didn't freeze over that first winter. And I guess Opal snuck out there and fed the child enough that it survived. What it come down to, Karl had a child he showed off to the world—and another child he hid away."

"Whoa!" I said. "Whatever happened to him?"

"Well, knowing what we know now? It might have been better to be that deformed boy in the silo than to have been Kyle. Because the things that happened to Kyle, they were worse than being left alone in a silo full of old corn."

"So did Karl . . . do things . . . to Kyle?"

"We don't really know, do we? All we know is what happened. I mean, a boy doesn't do a thing like that over nothing."

"But you just said . . ."

"Sometimes seeing a thing is worse than having a thing done to you. Do you see my meaning?"

"I'm not sure I do."

"Now we come to the part where Miss Hill enters the story. You see, Miss Hill had a special relationship with Kyle. There were people who said unkind things about the two of them back when Kyle was in school. People asking why it was that he stayed late after school with Miss Hill, things of that nature. But I believe Miss Hill had seen something dark and sad in that boy and she wanted to help.

"At any rate, the day Kyle was about to finish eleventh grade, Miss Hill went out to the farm where he lived to speak to his father and mother. You see, Kyle wanted to graduate from high school early, move to New York, try his hand in the music business. He already had a little combo that had played down the Cities a couple times. So Miss Hill went to Karl to tell him that Kyle was cut out for something different than growing corn in a small Minnesota town. Well, Karl listened to her without speaking. Then, when she was done, he said, 'My son is a farmer. He will stay a farmer.' Then he told Miss Hill that if she ever came back to his home, he would put an end to her life. I had a conversation with Miss Hill on this subject and she told me those were his exact words. 'I will put an end to your life.'

"Well, later that night, there was a call to the police station. It was Kyle Van Epps. He said that someone had killed his father. So Chief O'Donnell and the Sheriff went out there and what they found was so horrible it is hardly spoken of even now in this town."

"What *did* they find?"

"Well, they found his older brother, of course. He was still out there in that grain silo. Poor little fellow, with his twisted back and his doll arm. He had nothing but a little Japanese transistor radio out there. That and a piano. Lord only knows how or why a piano got into a grain silo. But there it was. They said when they came in, the radio was playing 'Love, Love Me Do' by the Beatles. They said they took him out of the silo and the boy wailed and cried something horrible. You see, he'd never seen the sun before. Never seen a tree. Never seen a house or a dog or a cow or a car. But the reason he was wailing and carrying on is that they took away his radio.

"But that wasn't all. They found a hole dug underneath the house. There was a cinder-block room made down there, with a little door in it so small you had to crawl in, and a chain fixed to the wall like you'd use to chain up a dog."

I felt queasy. I hate stuff like this. The second I come across one of these gross-out serial-killer documentaries on TV, I change the channel.

"Did he put Kyle down there?" Mrs. Krauthammer said. She shrugged. "Perhaps not. We know he put Opal down there. When the police arrived, she was chained under the house. According to what Miss Hill found out—which, admittedly was somewhat limited—Karl treated Kyle like the king of the roost. But if Opal did anything to displease Karl, he chained her up down there like a dog."

"So it was Kyle who did it?" I said. "Did Kyle kill his father?"

"The old man was found dead just outside the grain silo. But no weapon was ever found. And Kyle wouldn't speak about what happened. No charges were filed. Back in those days they tended to say that if a man deserved killing, there was no point in prosecuting whoever did it."

"So, what happened to the brother after Kyle left town?"

"Well, that's the big mystery, isn't it?"

"You tell me."

"After Kyle left town, they were supposed to put him in a state home. But the day that the gal from the state went down there, the place was empty. Opal was gone, Kyle was gone, the boy was gone. Later we heard Opal went back to her mother and father up in Hemming. But they say she didn't bring the boy with her. Opal died a year or two later. All that living under the house had broken her health. Soon after she died, a lawyer here in town received a letter from Kyle in New

York City. He told the lawyer to sell the farm and wire the money to him up in New York City. Apparently he instructed the lawyer to sell everything. One presumes that the money from the sale of the farm is what he used to buy that record company, Apex."

It occurred to me that if Kyle really had buried something on the farm—as Mom believed he had—then it was probably right around the farmhouse. "Is any of it still there? The house, the silo, any of that?"

"It all fell to rack and ruin. There's really nothing left of it now. If you drive out of town on State 14, you'll see a willow tree and the remains of the silo up on the hill to the left."

I thought about it for a minute. That must have been the place Mom was talking about, where she had dug looking for clues. I could see what she meant about the song. Thinking back about it, line by line, point by point, it matched up with the story Mrs. Krauthammer had just told me. Not that you could have used any of it in a court of law or anything. But if you'd known the story, the connections were unmistakable.

I pushed my hot chocolate away and stood up. It was killing me that I didn't know what was going on with Mom. "I have to go," I said.

# ELEVEN

**I LOOKED AT** the map Mrs. Krauthammer had given me. Mr. Osmund's house was on the way back to the apartment. I didn't care if the killer was still out here— I was going to check on Mom anyway. But since it was on the way, I figured I'd stop by Mr. Osmund's house. I knew I was taking a chance. If he *was* the killer, then I was in trouble. But I just couldn't really believe he was the guy. Mr. Osmund was a little shrimpy wimpy sour kind of guy. He just didn't seem like a murderer. But I figured I'd talk to him and see what he had to say for himself.

When I went outside, I noticed that the temperature had dropped. It had been in the twenties before. Cold, but not unbearable. But now it must have dropped well into the teens.

As I stumbled through the blinding snow, I heard something behind me. I couldn't see it in the whiteout. But I could hear it.

Footsteps.

"Hello?" I called. "Hello? Is somebody there?"

The sound of the footsteps stopped. Had I imagined it?

"I can hear you, you know," I said. I tried walking back toward where I'd last heard the sound. But floating in my bubble of falling gray flakes, I quickly lost my bearings.

I turned back in the direction I thought I was supposed to be going, and kept moving. Eventually I found a street sign, checked the map, kept going. I could still hear the footsteps behind me. Or I thought I could. But it didn't seem to make sense. If I couldn't see him—it seemed like it had to be a him, though I can't say why—then he couldn't see me. So how was he following me? The sound of my footsteps?

I tried to be as quiet as possible.

Still I could hear something behind me, something moving in the snow. What if it was the wolf? What if it was a whole pack of wolves? I felt a strange tingling feeling under my skin. I was trembling with fear. But on some level—this will sound weird—but on some level I was excited, too. I'd had this happen once or twice before in my life, this weird mixture of fear and euphoria. I felt like I was aware of everything around me, like every snowflake and every sound was pounding straight into my brain.

I moved as slowly and quietly as I could. I was going to fool them! I imagined that I was an Eskimo hunter moving through an icy wasteland as I hunted a huge polar bear. It was kind of freaky, really, how much I got into my little fantasy. I was almost totally lost in it. But without anything to look at but the snow, it was easy to lose track of reality.

One foot, step, ease the foot down into the snow. Stand. Wait. Listen. Move the other foot. Softly, softly, softly. Stop. Wait. Listen.

But despite my best efforts, whoever was trailing me, they were still there, I was sure of it.

Or . . . were they? With the wind whipping around me and the snow deadening the sounds of the world, I couldn't help thinking it was at least *possible* that the footsteps behind me were just my imagination.

But I didn't think so.

It must have taken me close to half an hour to make it to Mr. Osmund's house. I didn't make a wrong turn, I didn't trip, I didn't make any mistakes. I just moved slowly.

Mr. Osmund answered as soon as I rang the doorbell. He looked the same as ever: neat hair, neat gray mustache, wire-framed glasses with lenses so perfectly clean and unsmudged that they looked like they'd just come from the factory. Even though it was a Saturday, he wore a necktie under his gray V-neck cardigan. There was something taut and sad around his eyes, though, that was different from the way he looked at school.

He stared at me for a moment, then said, "Well. Come in, then."

Mr. Osmund's home, like his clothes, was exceedingly neat and without much character. His living room looked like a showroom at a moderate-priced furniture store. I halfway expected to see price tags hanging off the end tables.

"Could you lock the door?" I said.

Mr. Osmund nodded as though this wasn't an unusual request. After he'd locked the door, he joined me in the living room and sat down, back straight, palms flat on his knees.

"You heard?" I said.

"I heard you saw who did it."

I shook my head. "I saw a man. But in all that snow? No, I couldn't identify him."

I was studying Mr. Osmund, seeing if he reacted to what I had just said. He didn't. Not really. He just looked away from my face and stared at the far wall of his living room. Between a couple of cuckoo clocks hung framed pictures of his two dull, neat children graduating from the University of Minnesota, and one of those retouched family photos where everybody looks sort of blurry and plastic—Mr. Osmund, standing; Mrs. Osmund, bland and featureless, sitting; the two little Osmunds in their 1970s clothes smiling fearfully at the camera.

Mr. Osmund didn't say anything. But after a minute tears just started running down his face. I heard a sound behind me. Mr. Osmund's wife came out of the kitchen wearing an apron.

"Oh, stop it, Paul," she said. "Before I vomit." Then she turned to me, smoothed down her apron, and smiled. "May I offer you something to drink? Hot chocolate? Tea? Anything?"

"No, ma'am," I said. "I'm fine, thank you."

Mrs. Osmund looked at Mr. Osmund again, with an expression that I could only describe as disgust. *Okay,* I was thinking. *This is totally weird and uncomfortable!*

Mrs. Osmund's heels clicked away as she walked off toward the back of the house. When she was finally gone, Mr. Osmund took off his glasses, pulled out a very neat white handkerchief, and pressed it to his eyes.

"I apologize for that," he said. Then he put the handkerchief back in his pocket. He took a deep breath and straightened up. Other than the fact that his eyes were very red, he looked exactly like he always did, walking around the halls at school, writing kids up because they didn't have a hall pass. He pursed his lips. "Do you mind if I ask why you're here?"

"I'm trying to figure out who might have done this."

"Isn't that something better left to the police?"

"The last time I saw Chief Norgren, he had pretty much lost it. So, no, not really. Whoever did this is still out there. They already shot my mom, thinking she was me. I'd kinda like to figure out who it was before they finish the job and kill us both."

He blinked from behind his little glasses. "Is she . . ."

I shook my head. "No. She'll be okay, I think."

"I'm relieved to hear that." He put his hands on his forehead and stared at the ground for a moment. He seemed a little out of it.

"So . . ." I leaned toward him. "You seem pretty broken up about Miss Hill. I thought you hated her?"

"Why would you say that?"

"Everybody says you did."

Mr. Osmund's lips pursed slightly. "Miss Hill was an excellent teacher. We all respected her greatly."

"Oh!" I said, somewhat more sarcastically than I intended. "Well then!"

"That sort of attitude may fly in whatever place you came from, young lady," he said tartly. "But here in Greenville we—"

I interrupted him. "Hey, please, Mr. Osmund. Let me put this in simple words. I do not have time for this BS. A lady gets killed, you're crying, and your wife is looking at you like you just pooped in her Easter basket. How stupid do you think I am? Something's going on here."

Mr. Osmund stared at me. I got the impression he'd never had a kid go after him in quite that way. He looked totally flustered.

"My mom has just been shot," I said. "Fortunately she's not dead. For all I know, it was you who did it.

130

But I don't really think so. I think whoever shot her is the same person who shot Miss Hill. Now don't sit here and pretend she meant nothing to you. Don't sit here and pretend you don't know something more about Miss Hill than everybody else in this town does. Who would kill that lady? Why?"

Mr. Osmund took out his perfect handkerchief, blew his nose, put the handkerchief back in his pocket. It went back into the pocket slightly crooked. "Of course, of course," he said. "I suppose you're right."

But then he didn't say anything. So I just waited.

Finally he spoke. "They all think *I* did it, you know."

"Why?"

"Miss Hill and I had a . . . difficult relationship."

"Meaning what?"

"You saw my wife. Miss Hill and I . . ." He seemed to be struggling for words. "The first time I met Miss Hill, I thought, 'She's the one for me.' But she wasn't interested. I pursued her. But eventually I got the message. No interest. None. Zero." He sighed loudly. "Then I met Eileen. We were married. A few years later, Miss Hill and I went to a convention in Rochester. There were . . . indiscretions . . . between us. Stories circulated. Nothing happened between us, not really. A kiss. A little tasteless public groping. But that wasn't the point. Here I am, sixty-four years old, a year from retirement, and I still ... I'd be lying if I didn't admit that ... I still ... I still feel *something* for Miss Hill. And Eileen knows it." Mr. Osmund shook his head and looked at me intently. "My gracious, I don't know why in the world I'm telling this to a sixteen-year-old girl whom I barely know! I suppose it's because you're not from this place. You don't matter here."

*I didn't matter here.* In a way it was a really insulting thing to say. But I guess he was right. That was the thing that sucked about my life. No matter where I went, I didn't really matter. I had no roots, no attachments, no connections, no posse, no crew, no people.

"We don't have much time," I said. "We have to find out who did this. I think it has something to do with Kyle Van Epps."

A look of pain crossed his face. "Do you know what it's like when someone you care about is more interested in a sixteen-year-old boy than in you? It makes you feel ... insignificant."

"I'm not trying to be mean," I said. "Really. But I don't care how you feel. I just want to know who would have wanted to kill Miss Hill."

"Besides me?" He gave me a watery smile. "No one.

Everyone thought she was the bee's knees. The bee's knees. All the kids hate me. And they love her. They've always loved her. She insults them, she belittles them, she pushes them unmercifully. And still they love her." The watery smile faded and a look of bitterness came over his face. I wanted to say that it was obvious Miss Hill loved her kids. And it was obvious that he didn't, that he was just a guy doing a job.

"Kyle Van Epps," I said. "Could it have anything to do with Kyle Van Epps?"

Mr. Osmund looked up at me. "Kyle Van Epps? Why would it have anything to do with him?"

"I don't know," I said. "Did Miss Hill ever hear from him?"

"Miss Hill and I have not spoken in nearly ten years. How would I know?"

Ten years! Wow. They'd worked in the same building and never said a word in all that time. This was one angry old guy. "Everybody in this town seems to know everything about everybody. I'm guessing if she was in touch with Kyle Van Epps, you'd have heard."

He raised one eyebrow. "You are a very shrewd little girl," he said finally. "When I first saw you, I thought, 'Well, there goes a cute little airhead.' And, my word, how wrong I was."

I spread my hands. "Did she or didn't she?"

He narrowed his eyes. "Yes," he said finally. It was like he was squeezing a whole lifetime of frustration out with that one word.

"Kyle Van Epps was her first little protégé, her first little pet. She finds one every few years, some attractive young boy with a little talent and a pretty face. They come to her after school. Now she entices them with this little recording studio in her house. But back then, she just kept them after school and had them . . . I don't know . . . do music things, I suppose." He shrugged. "These days she helps them record all their awful teenage music, all their sappy little songs about how nobody appreciates their feelings and their talents." The way he said it, it was like poison was dripping out of his mouth.

"Was there anything beyond that?" I said. "Beyond . . . teaching."

"Oh, heavens, who knows! Certainly none of them ever complained. She was quite an attractive woman in her youth . . . but her youth is long gone. Maybe with Kyle. Maybe with a couple of the other early ones there was something improper. I can't say."

"Can't? Or won't?"

He looked at me sullenly. "Even in this town, my

dear, there are secrets. Even here, where everyone thinks they know everything about everyone . . . there are things that we will never know. All of us have our secret places. I'm sure she had hers. But I don't know them."

"What about Kyle? Was there anything different about him?"

"Different? Other than the fact that Kyle shot his father in cold blood just because he said something a little nasty to Miss Hill?"

"Do we know that?" I said. "Do we know it was him? Not the brother or the mother?"

"Oh, come on. The police felt sorry for him. He was the golden boy and he lived in a house of horrors, and so Chief O'Donnell and the county attorney claimed they had 'insufficient evidence for prosecution.' But everyone knew the truth. The boy got away with murder."

"Could it have been the mother, Opal? Or the crippled kid?"

Mr. Osmund closed his eyes. "I could have made her happy, you know," he said. "I *know* I could have."

*Great,* I thought. *Here we are back to his ancient crush on Miss Hill again.* It was like it was all he could think about.

"She always fell for the worst kind. Manipulators. Thieves. Liars. They could smell her a mile away." He shook his head again, like a boxer clearing away the cobwebs after a hard punch in the face. "And Kyle was the worst of them."

"Oh?"

"Miss Hill alibied him, you know." Mr. Osmund said it quietly. "She claimed that she was with him that night. At the time it happened."

"*With* her, with her? Like . . ."

Mr. Osmund looked a little rattled, like discussing sex with a kid made him nervous. Which, I guess, was normal. It made me feel a little odd, too. "No! Of course not. She just said that he was at the school copying an arrangement for the marching band."

I wondered why Mrs. Krauthammer had neglected to tell me this. Was it because she thought it was indelicate? She didn't seem like the delicate type. "How do you know this?"

"I heard it from Chief O'Donnell." Mr. Osmund narrowed his eyes. "She never saw them for what they were."

"You're saying you think she was lying when she alibied him."

"Of course she was! Kyle killed that man as sure as I'm standing here."

"Why? Because he didn't like his dad threatening

136

Miss Hill? Or because his father wouldn't agree to let him go to New York and pursue his dreams? Or was it one of those straw-that-broke-the-camel's-back things? His mother chained up under the house, his brother living in the silo, all that stuff?"

Mr. Osmund snorted. "Don't be ridiculous."

"What?" I said.

"Kyle Van Epps certainly wasn't protecting Miss Hill's honor. And I doubt he cared about all those terrible things his father was doing."

"Then what?"

"Money!"

"Money?" I said. The thought hadn't even entered my head.

"Money. Karl Van Epps was a very successful farmer. If you saw him in the street, you'd have thought he was just some old redneck with forty acres of poor soil. But he was quite a rich man. At that point he was probably worth somewhere in the neighborhood of a million dollars. That would be the equivalent of, oh, five or ten million today."

My eyes widened.

"Kyle Van Epps killed his father so he'd get all that land. I mean, his mother officially got the land. But I'm sure he thought he could control her. And then when she died? Well, that was that. And, by golly, the second her body was in the ground, the certified letter comes down from New York City. Sell the farm. And that, my dear, was the end of that."

"Huh," I said.

"Miss Hill has a very nice home," Mr. Osmund said. "She traveled every summer to expensive destinations. She bought her furniture in New York City. She bought clothes in Italy and France. She spent money on recording equipment, instruments, stereos, records, whatever she wanted—spent it as freely as water. I know what her salary was. Right down to the penny. No one could afford to do what she did on teacher's pay."

I stared at him. "What are you saying?"

He snorted like I was being stupid.

"You're saying she blackmailed him," I said.

"Blackmail. Hush money. A friendly contribution to her well-being. Call it whatever you want."

"What if she was threatening to expose him?" I said. "Maybe that's why she was killed."

Mr. Osmund rubbed his chin. "Why? Why after all these years?"

"I don't know. You tell me."

"I don't know either." He looked thoughtfully at the

ceiling. "It would make sense, though, wouldn't it? It would certainly give him motive to get rid of her."

What would have changed after all these years? I wondered. And I could only think of one thing. Me. Me and Mom. We had come to this town. *Oh, man,* I thought. *We have gotten that poor woman killed.* It was the only explanation that made sense. There were still a few missing pieces to put in place. But I felt sure I was onto something.

"What were you doing at ten o'clock this morning?" I said.

"Are you asking for *my* alibi?" he said.

I shrugged.

"I make cuckoo clocks," he said. "It's my hobby. I was in my shop out in the garage all morning, making the frame for a new clock."

Cuckoo clocks. That was pretty much perfect. I imagined him sitting there assembling the little mechanisms. Everything perfect, everything in order, no mess, no uncertainty, no unpredictability. It must have been as close to happiness as this guy ever got.

I stood up. "I'm sorry," I said. "I'm sorry for what you're going through." I didn't really like Mr. Osmund. But I did feel sorry for him. All these years, pining away after some woman who didn't care for him. It was kind of pathetic.

Mr. Osmund looked up at me sharply. "You're a girl," he said. "What did those boys have that I don't? Is it just looks? Or is it something else?"

I looked over at the picture of Mr. Osmund with his family, the one taken back in the seventies. He really wasn't a bad-looking guy back then.

"You really want to know?" I said.

He stared at me for a long time.

I wanted to say, *Look, what's the point of life if you can't bust loose and have some fun every now and then?* The poor guy had no fun, no enthusiasm, no laughter, no joy, no mischief in him. I bet if you'd looked at Mr. Osmund's coloring books from when he was a kid, he wouldn't have colored outside the lines, not even once. And Miss Hill couldn't stand a guy like that.

But what could I say? Nothing that wouldn't make the guy feel even worse.

"I don't know," I said. "It's hard to see inside a person's heart."

# TWELVE

**INSTEAD OF LEAVING** through Mr. Osmund's front door, I decided to sneak out the back. Whoever had been following me—*if* there was somebody following me—they'd probably be waiting for me out front.

As I was about to let myself out the back door, Mrs. Osmund spotted me and said, "I'm sorry, sweetheart."

"About what?"

"That scene I made before." Mrs. Osmund had

taken off the apron she was wearing before. She wore a sweater with little beads and buttons stitched onto it, and she had what I call "beauty-parlor hair"—a sort of stiff helmet of curls that glistened with hairspray.

I shrugged. "Hey, look . . ."

"No." She pursed her lips. "It was wrong of me. I'm afraid I'm not very good at forgiveness."

"Look . . ." I said again.

Mrs. Osmund stepped between me and the door. "My husband is a good man. We all have our weaknesses. Miss Hill was his."

"Sure."

The Osmunds' house seemed full of regrets and sadness, and, *man,* did I want to get out of there. But it seemed like there was something Mrs. Osmund wanted to tell me. "Is there something else?" I said.

"No, no," she said. "Just that. I just wanted to apologize."

"Okay. Well. I probably need to go."

But Mrs. Osmund didn't move. "He's a good man. A good father. A good husband. I just want you to know that. He would never do anything . . ." She waved her hand vaguely in the air.

"Sure." I nodded.

Finally she stepped aside. I pulled the door open.

Something occurred to me, a question I should ask, just to cover all the bases.

"So, what you're saying..." I tried to think of a tactful way to say it. "So did Mr. Osmund go out this morning?"

"In *this* weather?" she said.

"I was just curious," I said. I decided to push a little, tell a white lie. "I thought I saw him on Broad Street a couple hours ago."

She frowned. "No. No, I'm sure you're mistaken. He's got a new clock going. When he gets started on a clock, there's no stopping him."

I smiled. "I bet," I said.

Then I slipped out into the snow. I was desperate to find out how Mom was doing.

Alone again. Cold, gray, the world fading into frigid indistinct nothingness.

I don't know what it was, but every time I went out into the storm, I got more nervous about it. The first time I went out, it was interesting in a slightly spooky way. But now I was sick of it. The numb, isolated feeling of being in the middle of a vast expanse of nothingness had lost all its charm. Now I just felt scared and sick. Snow World. Now I just wanted to get out of it.

Katie met me at the door of our apartment. She had a grim look on her face. "We couldn't find the doctor. He's out of town or something."

I looked behind her. Mom was lying on the couch now. There was an alarming amount of blood on the floor where she'd first fallen. Fabe was trying to clean it up with a towel, but he seemed to be mostly just smearing it around.

"I have an idea," I said. Everybody looked at me. "But we'll have to carry her."

"Carry her?" Katie said. "Carry her where?"

"Don't worry about that right now," I said. "Fabe, do you think you could carry her, I don't know, maybe six or eight blocks?"

"In this snow?" Fabe is a big strong guy. But he looked dubious about the idea. "I mean, maybe I could . . ."

Now that I thought about it, it didn't seem very smart. Mom would get banged around and—

"What about a stretcher?" Katie said.

"We don't have a stretcher," I said.

She pointed at the bathroom door. "Take that off its hinges. She could lie on it."

"That might work."

Fabe went over to the door. "Have you got a screw-driver?" he said. "I'll need to pry the hinge pins out."

"How about this?" Katie said. She lifted her foot in the air and stomped on the door. It tore the hinges right out of the cheap wood frame.

"Or we could do that," Fabe said.

"Get her on the door," I said. "Put some blankets on her."

"What are you doing?" Mom said. She seemed only vaguely aware of what was going on.

"We're getting you some help," I said.

Within minutes Mom was lying on the door, swaddled in every blanket I could find. Katie and I got in front and Fabe got in the back. We started creeping down the stairs outside the house. To keep Mom from slipping off the door, Katie and I had to hold her over our heads while Fabe stooped over.

"Careful!" I said. "If anybody slips—" I didn't finish the sentence. It was obvious that if anybody slipped on the icy steel stairs, any or all of us could get badly hurt—Mom being the most vulnerable.

There were a couple of close shaves, but we made it. The wind was howling around us.

"Where are we going?" Katie said.

"North Myrtle," I said. "I think it's that way."

Katie narrowed her eyes thoughtfully. "I think we should go that way." She pointed into the gray emptiness.

We looked at Fabe. "Don't ask me," he said. "It's not my town."

"We'll go your way," I said to Katie. Fabe was right. It *was* her town. She was more likely to be right than me.

Mom moaned. The wind snatched at the covers over her. I didn't want her out here any longer than necessary. Every minute out in this miserable cold was sucking the life out of her already weakened body. "Let's go," I said.

We headed into the swirling gray nothingness of Snow World. The snow was deeper now, probably a good foot deep. Sometimes we'd hit drifts that were a lot deeper. The hard edges of the door were cutting into my hand. Mom wasn't moving. Around us, nothing changed. It felt like we were on some kind of nightmarish arctic treadmill, stumbling on and on, but getting nowhere.

After we'd gone what seemed a long way, I started to feel tears running down my face. Now that we were out here, I started feeling like I'd made a terrible mistake. We were going to get lost and Mom was going to die and it was all going to be my fault.

"Hey!" Katie said to me. "Stop that!"

But I couldn't help it. It was all catching up with me—Mom, Miss Hill, the cold, the snow, the feeling of being trapped in this town with nowhere to run . . .

I felt like just quitting, like just lying down in the snow and giving up.

But then Fabe started singing. I'd never heard him sing before. His speaking voice was a deep baritone. But guys who don't sing often don't know how to use their adult voices and keep singing in high childish voices like they did before their voices changed. That was Fabe.

His singing would have been kind of comical under any other circumstances. But right now there was something sweet—almost angelic about it.

"Row, row, row your boat," he started singing, "gently down the stream . . ."

Katie jumped in, too. ". . . merrily, merrily, merrily, merrily, life is but a dream."

"Come on," Fabe said to me. Then he started singing again.

For a minute I wanted to punch them both. This

was serious! And here they were trying to cheer me up with some dumb kindergarten song. This time they started singing it as a round, Fabe first, then Katie.

The tears were just running down my face.

Then a third voice cut in. It was Mom. Her eyes were closed and her voice was so quiet you could barely hear it under the howling of the wind. But still, she'd once been a professional singer, and she still had the pipes to cut through the wind.

"Row, row, row your boat gently down the stream . . ."

Hey, what could I do? If you can't beat 'em, join 'em. I started singing, too. We went once through the round and then we bumped into a sign. Woodland Street. We were moving in the right direction.

We got turned around once, walked through somebody's backyard, ran into a car—but we were moving in the right direction. And we kept singing.

Somewhere along the way Mom's voice dropped out. But the rest of us kept going.

Then, on the next street, someone appeared out of the snow. It was a boy from the middle school. When he saw what we were doing, he didn't freak out, he just said, "Where you trying to get her to?"

"Mrs. Krauthammer's house over on North Myrtle," I said.

He disappeared into the snow. "I'll get help," he said.

I figured that was the last we'd see of him. But then a man in a big parka appeared. He didn't say anything, he just started singing along with us, joining Fabe's part with a deep bass voice, an octave below the rest of us. He nudged Katie aside and took her corner of the door.

"This way!" someone yelled. "Follow my voice!"

I don't know who it was. It was just somebody from the town.

People started appearing out of the gray emptiness, singing, joining in with the parts. Nobody asked questions or made comments, they just sang. And ahead of us I could hear voices: "What street are we on?" "Which way to North Myrtle?" "What's your address?" "Which way's north?" "That way." "Over here." "Go this way."

The crowd around us got bigger and bigger. Somebody started singing a harmony baritone part. Then somebody else chimed in on alto. Two-part harmony turned into three-part harmony. I don't want to give you the impression it was the Mormon Tabernacle

Choir. It wasn't. But still, there was something amazing and beautiful about it.

Pretty soon there were six or seven people, most of them men, holding the edges of the door. It had gotten so light that I was barely carrying any weight.

"This way! This way!" someone was calling out of the snow.

And then we turned and the dark form of a house swam up out of the snow. Mrs. Krauthammer stood on the porch, snowflakes melting in her white hair and on her wide shoulders.

My face burned from the heat as we carried Mom inside.

"On the table," Mrs. Krauthammer commanded, pointing at the sturdy old formal table in her dining room. The men laid Mom where Mrs. Krauthammer pointed. Her blood had stained the sheets and blankets we'd wrapped around her. Her eyes were closed and her face was an awful bluish color.

Outside I heard the roar of a snowmobile's engine. A man came running up the front porch steps and burst into the room. He was carrying several clear plastic IV bags, gauze, and some other things. "I busted into Dr. Saarsgard's office and got these," he said.

Mrs. Krauthammer looked around the room. It seemed like about half the people in Greenville had drifted into her house.

"That will be all," Mrs. Krauthammer said. "I thank you for your help, but this is now a surgical theater, not a movie theater."

Heads nodded and people began filing out the front door. Fabe closed the door after them.

"Everyone wash your hands and glove up," Mrs. Krauthammer commanded after the door was closed. I went into the kitchen, scrubbed my hands as thoroughly as possible, then pulled on a pair of latex surgical gloves from a box on the table. Fabe, Katie, and Mrs. Krauthammer did the same.

Mrs. Krauthammer quickly cut Mom's blouse off with a pair of surgical shears and then began putting an IV into a vein in Mom's arm. I noticed that Mrs. Krauthammer's hands were trembling.

"Darn it!" she said. Apparently she had missed the vein.

"Are you okay?" I said.

"Pour me some whiskey," she said grimly.

"Is that really going to—"

"Just do it!" she said.

I poured the whiskey while she attempted to get the needle into Mom's arm. It took her four tries. But she finally got there.

"Here," she said to Fabe, handing him an IV bag that said SALINE on the side. "Squeeze it gently. She's lost a lot of blood. We've got to push fluids into her or we'll lose her to shock."

I handed Mrs. Krauthammer a plastic cup full of whiskey. I thought she was going to drink it. But instead she poured it over the bullet hole in Mom's shoulder. "They didn't bring any Betadine," she said. "We need to sterilize the wound. Young lady . . ." She turned to Katie. "Go into my medicine chest down the hall. There's a tube of antibiotic ointment. Go get it."

"Yes, ma'am," Katie said, running down the hallway.

"You're going to be my assistant," the old nurse said to Fabe. "My hands are not very steady, so I may ask you to do some things that are quite hard. Don't think. Just do them."

Fabe said, "Look, um, I'm not so great with blood. I'm kinda . . ." He looked down at the blood oozing out of Mom's shoulder. "I have to sit down," he said. He shoved the IV bag into my hand. Then he just sort of collapsed onto the couch.

"Hmmph!" Mrs. Krauthammer said. "The scary-looking ones are always the biggest sissies." Then she turned to me. "So it's up to you."

"What is?"

"I have Parkinson's disease," she said. "Just the early stages. But I can't . . ." She held up her hand. It trembled uncontrollably.

"Just tell me what to do," I said.

Katie showed up with the antibiotic ointment. "You," Mrs. Krauthammer said, pointing to Katie, "with all the metal protruding from your head, squeeze the bag." I handed Katie the IV bag.

Mrs. Krauthammer opened the grocery bag full of medical supplies, started taking things out and setting them in a row on the table. "This isn't a suitably sterile surgical field," she said. "But sometimes one is forced to improvise."

I couldn't help noticing that one of the things she set on the table was a scalpel. Another was a large hook-shaped needle.

"So, uh, what exactly are we doing?" I said.

"There's an artery deep in her shoulder that's bleeding," Mrs. Krauthammer said, sponging off the area with more whiskey. "You'll have to cut down to it, and tie it off. Then you'll suture the wounds shut."

"What!" I said. I was feeling like I was going to be joining Fabe in the Fainting-and-Falling-on-the-Floor Club.

"Keep squeezing, young lady," she said to Katie.

"The scalpel," Mrs. Krauthammer said, pressing the scalpel into my hand. "If you can cut a piece of chicken, you can do surgery. Now, what you'll need to do is—"

"I can't," I said.

"Young lady, do you want your mother to survive?" she demanded.

But I didn't answer. I literally couldn't move. I just stood there staring at the hole in Mom's shoulder. It was really freaking me out.

Katie nudged me gently. "It'll be easier for me," she said. "She's not my mom." She handed the IV bag back to me, took the scalpel from Mrs. Krauthammer, and said, "Just tell me where."

I couldn't watch. I turned my back and kept squeezing the bag while Mrs. Krauthammer said, "Cut there. Just like . . . good . . . yes . . . deeper, hon, deeper."

After a minute I just started singing. I don't even know what I sang, but I figured anything that would keep my mind off what Mrs. Krauthammer was saying would be better than joining Fabe on the couch.

"That's very pretty," Mrs. Krauthammer said. "You just keep singing."

I sang while Katie operated on my mother. It seemed like it took forever. As best I could tell from the way Mrs. Krauthammer was talking, it was more complicated than she had expected, and things kept going wrong. But I could also tell the problems weren't Katie's fault. It was just the nature of the situation.

"You're doing magnificently, Katie," Mrs. Krauthammer kept saying. "Magnificently. Good. Now tie that off. Just like I showed you. The same knot. Good. Good. Superb."

I sang Johnny Cash. I sang the Clash. I sang John Mayer. I sang folk songs and rock songs and hymns and Handel.

After a while Fabe stood up. "I'm sorry," he said. "But I just can't—" He waved his hand vaguely at the surgery that was going on behind us. Then he went onto the front porch and paced up and down outside for a while.

Mrs. Krauthammer changed IVs four times during the surgery. Which indicated Mom had lost four quarts of blood. Without the saline, Mrs. Krauthammer told me, Mom would have died.

*Thanks,* I thought. *Could have skipped that piece of information and I'd have been just fine.*

But finally it was over.

Mrs. Krauthammer pulled the blanket up over the fresh bandage on Mom's chest.

"Is she going to be okay?" I said.

"Thanks to your friend here, yes," Mrs. Krauthammer said. Then she turned away. "I'm going to go get some fresh linens."

Katie's shirt was covered with blood. She was standing there stock-still with this blank expression on her face.

"I'm sorry you had to do that, Katie," I said.

Katie said nothing. She had the oddest look in her eyes.

Mrs. Krauthammer walked slowly down the hallway, leaning on her cane.

"I just couldn't do it," I said. "I'm sorry."

Katie's eyes were wide and glistening. "Oh, man," she said finally. "Oh, man. Oh, man, I can't believe it. I just can't believe it."

"It's okay," I said. "You did great. I'm sorry."

She took off her surgical gloves—*snap! snap!*—and dropped them unconsciously on the floor. Then she started rubbing her face, rubbing and rubbing like she was trying to get something off of it.

"I'm sorry," I said again. "Nobody should have to—"

"No, it's not that!" she said. She had this strange look in her eyes, like somebody had just handed her a million dollars, and she couldn't quite believe it. "Is it . . ." She hesitated. "Would it be . . ."

"What?" I said.

"Is there something wrong with me?"

*"What?"* I said again.

"I don't know quite how to say this," she said hesitantly. Her voice was low, awestruck. "But that was the coolest thing I've ever done in my life."

I stared at her.

"I mean . . . seriously. I just feel like . . . *pow!*" She put her hand on my arm. "You remember how you told me once that the first time you picked up a guitar, you knew what you were going to do with your life?"

"Sure."

"I felt that way just now. I mean, I've got this knife in my hand and I'm cutting . . . I'm cutting human flesh! And I'm like . . . dude, I'm like, man, this is freakin' *it*! You know?" She kept rubbing her face. "What's wrong with me?"

"Hey, Katester, you can feel any way you want," I said. "But you just saved my mother's life."

She stared at me. She blinked. She blinked again. Then this huge grin split her face. "Yeah, I did, didn't I?"

I couldn't help laughing.

"I just did *surgery,* dude!" she said. She grabbed my shoulder and shook it. "I just did surgery!"

We were interrupted by Fabe's voice. "Uh, Chass?" He was poking his head in the front door. "Chass, I think you better come out here."

# THIRTEEN

I RAN OUT the front door.

"Look," Fabe said.

It didn't take long to see what he was pointing at. For the first time in hours, the snow had slackened. In fact, it was barely coming down at all. On the horizon smoke was drifting upward, losing itself in the gray sky.

"What is it?" I said.

Katie came out from behind me. "It's the high school!" she said.

She was right. I could see the green roof of the two-story building peeping over the trees. No flames were visible, but a lot of smoke was pouring out of the vents in the roof.

"The instruments!" Katie said. "All the band instruments are gonna get burned up."

I have to admit, it didn't seem like the end of the world if my piccolo got melted into a puddle of molten metal. But what occurred to me was that if somebody had set fire to the building, there was probably something there that they didn't want anybody to find. Some sort of clue that might lead back to the killer.

Katie charged out into the street and began leaping through the powdery snow. I turned and saw Mrs. Krauthammer walking slowly down the stairs, carrying a bunch of clean sheets. "Is Mom going to be okay?" I said.

"The best thing we can do is to leave her right where she is," Mrs. Krauthammer said. She added, "She'll be fine with me. Go do what you need to do." She walked to the mantel, took down an old shotgun. "If anybody comes, I know how to use this."

"I'll stay with your mom and Mrs. Krauthammer," Fabe said. "You go do what you need to do."

"Okay," I said, pulling on my coat. I ran out the front door and followed Katie's footprints in the snow.

The school was a squat, ugly, two-story brick building that must have been built about fifty years ago. By the time I got there, there were still no flames visible—but heavy black smoke was pouring out of vents in all the eaves.

Katie was right in front of me.

"The door's locked," she shouted.

"Help me," I said, grabbing one side of a heavy metal trash can.

Katie immediately recognized what I had in mind. We grabbed the trash can and smashed it several times into the glass door. On the third blow, the glass shattered.

"Let's go!" Katie shouted.

I followed her into the building. The air was heavy with acrid smoke. For a moment I thought maybe this was a dumb idea. But Katie was already racing down the hallway. I followed as she ran up the stairs to the second floor.

Soon we were in the band room. For the first time I could see flames. One entire wall of the room was burning. Rows of instruments were stacked up on the opposite side of the room. Theoretically all the kids were supposed to take their instruments home. But this weekend the concert band was supposed to play in a contest and lots of kids had left them at school to pick up when the bus left for the contest. Obviously the contest had been canceled because of the weather. So more than half of the instruments were stacked up in the back of the room.

Katie ran over and started grabbing all the smallest instruments—flutes, clarinets, things like that—and stacking them up in my arms. I scanned the room, looking for something that seemed out of place. Like I said, the instruments weren't a big priority with me at that moment.

"You take them," I said.

Katie gave me a funny look.

"I need to check on something," I said.

"But—"

I didn't give her time to protest. I handed all the instrument cases back to her, then ran toward Miss Hill's office, which was in the back corner, near where the flames were coming from. I ran toward them. The heat was so strong it felt like my face would blister. I ducked through the doorway into Miss Hill's office. It was full of smoke—but it wasn't on fire yet.

I noticed that a filing cabinet in the back of the room was open. I pulled the hood of my parka across my face to try to filter the smoke. It helped a little—but not much—as I looked into the open drawer. It was empty.

I saw that the floor was covered with file folders. The names of kids were on the folders. I picked one up. *Dewey Newman.* He was the worst trumpet player in the band. I flipped the folder open. There were some sheets with grades recorded on them, a few music-theory test papers, a few other odds and ends. Nothing interesting.

Somebody had been in this office. Somebody who was looking for something.

I kicked at the pile of folders. All of them were marked with names of students. *Carrie Norman. Justine Lake. Elliot Krieghoff.* There was no way I'd be able to find anything of value in the few short minutes I had in here.

"Help, Chass!" Katie yelled. "I can't get the French horns!"

"In a minute!" I shouted back. I love a French horn

as much as the next guy . . . but that just wasn't my top priority at that moment.

What else? What else? I probed the smoky room looking for a clue. Maybe they'd found whatever they wanted. But if that was the case, why set the place on fire? No, there had to be something still here, something they wanted destroyed.

I pulled out the drawers to Miss Hill's desk. Rubber bands, string, pencils, musical staff paper. But nothing vaguely resembling a reason for torching a school.

I heard a loud clatter and a scream from the other room. My heart jumped. I ran out the door back into the band room. The shelves on the far wall had collapsed. And Katie was trapped under piles of tuba cases and trombones and shelving.

I ran over and grabbed her arm. A jet of fire ran up the far wall. It struck me as kind of ironic that I'd been on the verge of freezing to death all day—and here we were about to get killed in a fire.

"Help me!" Katie called. "I think I did something to my ankle!"

I grabbed her hand and yanked her to her feet. My heart was pounding and the heat was so intense I was afraid I wasn't going to be able to stand it much longer.

The smoke was stronger, too, and I could barely see the way out of the room.

"Let's go," I said.

"But what about the—"

"Forget about the instruments," I said. "You did what you could."

Supporting Katie's weight, I plunged through the smoke and out the door. Katie was grimacing with every step.

The flames had spread and now the hallway was engulfed in fire. "There's the door," I said. I wasn't sure we'd be able to get through it, the fire was so intense.

"I won't be able to make it," Katie said. "You'll have to sprint to get to the door."

I realized she was right. "I'm not leaving you," I said.

"But—"

"Forget it." I turned and steered her in the opposite direction, heading toward the front of the school. We had a long way to go before we'd get to any outside doors. I just had to hope that the fire wouldn't be quite as intense in this direction.

We hobbled past Mr. Arvid's English classroom and down toward the front of the building. At first I thought we'd be okay. But then when we reached the stairwell, I saw we were in trouble again. A gout of flame was shooting out of the stairwell. If anything, it was worse than the fire back in the band room. Whoever set the fire must have lit several parts of the building. They were sure determined to burn this place down!

"What about a window?" Katie said.

"Last resort," I said grimly. "If you jump on that ankle, you won't be walking for a year."

"Better that than burning to death!" Katie said. Then she gasped and winced. "Then again, maybe you're right!" A thin smile spread briefly across her face.

We headed back up the hallway. The smoke was so strong it was making it hard to breathe.

"More people die in fires from smoke inhalation than from heat," Katie said.

"Thanks for that," I said. "Any other cheery facts about dying in fires that you want to share?"

"Not that I can think of," she said.

There was a second stairwell, smaller than the main stairwell, tucked into the back of the school. Katie pointed toward it. We'd have to pass some fire on the way . . . but it seemed like our best hope.

I struggled to haul her down the hallway. Flames were jumping out toward us, but we kept pushing on. I had this panicky, trapped feeling. But finally we made it. The stairwell was almost completely free of smoke.

"Maybe we should just stay here," Katie said as we slammed the heavy metal door shut behind us.

I shook my head. "We'll just get trapped. We have to keep going."

Katie stopped and sat down. "I'm too tired," she said. "I just need to rest for a sec."

"Get up!" I shouted. "You have to keep going."

She sighed heavily. "Okay, okay!"

She grimaced as she got to her feet and began bouncing slowly down, step after painful step. As we reached the bottom there was a hollow boom somewhere in the building.

"What was *that*?" she said.

I didn't say anything. But I think we both knew. Some part of the building had just collapsed. We needed to get out *now*.

"Just hurry," I said.

She kept going, step after step. It seemed to take her forever. But there wasn't really much I could do to speed things up.

Finally she reached the bottom. I opened the steel door. The entire hallway was full of smoke and it was suddenly very hard to breathe. I couldn't see flames—

but there was a sickly orange glow seeping through the heavy gloom.

Suddenly I saw a shadow move in front of the orange light. A figure of a man.

"Who's there?" I shouted.

But there was no answer.

Katie turned to me. "Did you see it?" she whispered.

I nodded.

"Hey! Over here! Help us out!" she called.

The shadow appeared again, then disappeared. There was something furtive about the way the shadow moved—like whoever it was didn't want to be seen.

"He came out of the principal's office!" Katie whispered.

"Maybe we can get out that way," I said. "Isn't there a door in the back of the administration area?"

"I don't know," she said.

I urged her forward. The hallway seemed unnaturally calm. It was really, really hot. But where were the flames? It was also nearly impossible to breathe—not just from the layer of smoke hovering a few feet off the ground, but because it seemed like all the oxygen had been burned out of the air. I crouched and shuffled forward, panting and trying to stay below the worst air.

As we reached the door with PRINCIPAL'S OFFICE stenciled on it, I heard something at the far end of the hallway—a screech of metal on metal. Someone had just opened a door.

And just like that, the entire hallway was on fire. I think it's called flashover or flame-over or something like that—the point where all the flammable crap in the air suddenly gets enough oxygen to ignite. The only thing that saved us was that the old school had been built in the days when schools had twelve-foot ceilings. The flames raced across the ceiling in a voracious *WHOOOOOSH!* as oxygen entered through the open door at the end of the hallway. I could literally see the flames racing down the hallway toward us.

Katie screamed.

Hey, I probably screamed, too—I couldn't tell you. All I know is that I shoved Katie through the door into the principal's office. She hit the ground, clutching her foot, as I slammed the door behind us.

If you hadn't known better, you'd have thought nothing was wrong. There was no smoke in the office, no fire, no nothing. The lights were on and a radio was playing this sappy song from the sixties, "Do You Know the Way to San Jose?" The song was drenched in cheery horns and gloopy strings and glockenspiels and stuff. It just seemed so ridiculous in the middle of this craziness that I felt like laughing.

But I didn't. I was too freakin' scared!

Katie lay on the floor, holding up her hand toward me, this strange expression on her face.

"What?" I said.

It looked like her hand was wet. I saw then that there was water all over the floor. For a second I figured maybe it was water from the sprinkler system. It was only then that it struck me that I hadn't seen any sprinklers in operation. Certainly not in the office. So where did all the water come from?

"Gas," she whispered. "There's gas everywhere."

I guess the smoke had dulled my sense of smell, because I hadn't noticed the odor until she had pointed out the gasoline. The floor glistened. A discarded gas can lay over in the corner of the room.

"If those flames get through this door," Katie said, "this whole place is gonna go like a bomb."

"We've gotta get out," I said. "Now!"

I hoisted Katie to her feet, propelled her around the front counter, through the area where the school secretary's desk sat, and into Mr. Osmund's office.

Katie pointed over my shoulder. There was a storeroom off to the side of Mr. Osmund's office, its shelves full of books. At the far end of the room was a door with a red sign that said EXIT over it.

I charged into the other room, pressed the steel bar that opened the door. Only . . . the door barely budged.

It was chained shut!

Katie saw it the moment I did.

"Oh my God!" she said.

"We need something to bust it open," I said. "A crowbar or something."

"In here," Katie said, pointing. I ran back in to see what she was pointing at. As I rounded the desk, I noticed something strange. Mr. Osmund's computer looked like someone had been beating on it. The screen was smashed and the metal case of the computer itself was dented and broken. A couple of CD-ROMs lay on the desk, most of them smashed to bits. They all had handwritten labels scrawled on them. It looked like they had been used to back up the data on the computer. On the desk next to the broken CD-ROMs was the item Katie was pointing at—a large claw hammer.

"Bust the lock with that!" she shouted.

I grabbed the hammer, ran back into the storeroom, and started whaling away at the cheap little lock that held the links of chain together.

It didn't take but about three or four blows. The

lock broke in half and fell on the floor. I unwrapped the chain and shoved the door open.

"Go!" I shouted.

Katie stampeded past me. Outside the snow looked so calm and peaceful—a bizarre contrast after the fiery interior of the school.

A ring of people stood around the building, staring and pointing. There were a ton of kids from the school.

"Hurry!" one kid shouted. I recognized her. It was Justine Chaudry. Near her stood half the girls on the cheerleading squad. Coach Lacey, the girls' basketball coach stood beside them.

"Get out of there, girls!" he shouted. "The whole thing's about to come down."

I don't know why, but for a second I hesitated. Then I ran back inside the school.

"What are you *doing*?" Katie's voice pursued me as I tore through the storeroom and back into Mr. Osmund's office.

I wasn't really sure why I was doing it—not until I got back into the office. "Do You Know the Way to San Jose?" was still playing, the horns going *ba-pa-ba ba-bup-bup-ba-ba-BAAAAA*. And then I realized what it was. I'd come in here because I figured whoever burned this place was trying to hide something. Suddenly it seemed blindingly obvious what that something was. It was something that was on the administration's computer. Why else would they have smashed up all those disks with the backup data on them?

Maybe it was some kid with a grudge against the school. Somebody who was trying to hide a bad grade? Or some bad test results? It seems stupid looking back at it—but it teed me off that somebody would burn down our school over something like that. I knew I couldn't get the computer itself. Were there still a few CD-ROMs left that hadn't been destroyed? Maybe whatever they were trying to hide had been on one of them.

I searched the desk. There was only one unsmashed disk. I slipped it under my coat and hauled butt out of the school.

As I was running across the snow, I heard this *WHUMMPPHH!* noise. A jet of flame came shooting out the door behind me like someone had lit a humongous blowtorch. I could feel the heat on my back. But I didn't stop. I just kept running.

Finally I reached the ring of onlookers. They were all staring at me.

"Hey," I said. "It's okay. I made it."

"Uh," Katie said. "Yeah. But you're kind of on fire . . ."

# FOURTEEN

IT DIDN'T TAKE long to put the fire out. It was only the back of my parka. I rolled on the ground a couple of times and then took my coat off and whacked it in the snow. When I was done, it was smoking a little and there was a small patch of melted polyester on the back. But the fire was out. It really didn't look like that big a deal.

"I'm fine," I said. "I'm cool."

"Ohmygod!" Justine Chaudry said.

"You were like on *fire*!" one of the other cheerleaders said.

"Hey," I said. "It's no big deal." I was trying so hard to be cool, you wouldn't believe it.

"Dude, you were *totally* on fire!" said a kid I knew from algebra class.

As I was putting my jacket on (did I mention that it was freakin' *cold* out there?), Mr. Osmund came around the corner, followed by a couple members of the volunteer fire department. They were all smudged with smoke, Mr. Osmund included. There were white tracks running down Mr. Osmund's blackened face, like he'd been crying.

"Thank God, you're okay!" he shouted. "Is anyone else in there?"

Katie and I exchanged glances. Now that we were out, the whole experience seemed a little surreal. Had there really been somebody in there? Had there really been a shadow moving in that hallway?

Before I had a chance to say anything, Katie shook her head. "Nobody was there. Just us. We were trying to save the band instruments. But we got cut off."

Mr. Osmund stared at us. "You went into a burning building just to save a couple of flutes?" he said. "That's crazy!"

"Mr. Osmund," one of the volunteer firefighters said, "we're having trouble with the water pressure. We can get enough water to save part of the building. But not the whole thing. You need to make a decision. Right now."

I noticed something gleaming in the snow. The CD that I'd taken out of Mr. Osmund's office. I ran over and picked it up, then turned back to give it to Mr. Osmund. I figured he'd know what to do with it.

But when I turned around to give it to him, he was already walking away with the firefighters.

As I tucked the CD back into the pocket of my singed coat, I saw one of the cheerleaders look over at Katie and say, "What a weirdo. Risking her life over a bunch of flutes."

"Looks like that Chass girl saved her bacon, huh?" Justine said.

"I know," another girl said. "Metalface would probably be dead if it weren't for her!"

Metalface—that's what a lot of the kids called Katie because of the studs she wore in her nose and lips. It seemed sad to me; for some reason they seemed to think I was okay ... but they felt like they could say any nasty thing they wanted about Katie, and it didn't matter.

I went over and sat on the snow next to Katie. She was holding her ankle, staring at the burning building, tears running down her face.

"Why do they do that?" she said. "I mean they know I can hear them."

I shook my head. "I don't know. They're jerks."

A large snowflake landed on Katie's cheek. It melted. Then another hit her eyelash. She squinted, blinked. The snowflake went away. "Who do you think that was in the building?"

I shook my head. "It looks like they were trying to mess up the secretary's computer. Maybe we got this whole thing wrong. Maybe it's just about grades."

"You think somebody actually burned this place down over *grades*?"

I shrugged. "I've heard of people doing worse things over nothing."

She cocked her head. The snow had started falling harder again. "Worse things?"

"Miss Hill," I said. "Whoever did this—they probably killed Miss Hill, too."

Katie's eyes widened. "Do you think . . ."

"What?" I said.

"Well . . . something just occurred to me."

"What?"

She stood up and tried to walk. Her leg seemed to give out on her and she collapsed on the ground. "Ow!" she howled. Her face had gone white as a sheet. "I've got an idea," she panted. "But I think I need to get somewhere I can lie down."

As we were talking, I heard a roar behind us. A snowmobile had just pulled into the field where we were standing. "Hey!" I shouted. "Over here!"

The driver of the snowmobile saw me signaling and cut the handlebars of the big machine. It whirled around and headed toward us. As it pulled up next to us, I recognized the driver. It was Elliot Krieghoff, the son of the old creep who owned our apartment and the snow-mobile dealership under it. Like his father, he was a very handsome guy. And, also, like his father, there was something shifty-looking about him.

He climbed off the snowmobile and grinned. "Hey, my dad about had a fit this morning," he said. "I hear you stole one of his sleds and then trashed it some-where."

"Uh . . ." I said.

"Hey, what do I care?" he said. "My old man's an A-hole." He looked at Katie. "Dude, she doesn't look so great."

"Yeah," I said. "I need some help. You think you

could take her back to her house? I think she may have broken her ankle."

"No!" Katie said. She sounded strangely vehement. I'd noticed that Katie did pretty much everything she could to avoid spending time in her own home. She lived in a trailer on the south side of town with her mother and her older brother. Her mom seemed to have a cigarette permanently glued to her lip, and her brother had crude tattoos of Nazi-looking stuff on his neck.

"Wait," I said, "I've got a better idea. Let's take her to Mrs. Krauthammer's place. She's a nurse. Maybe she can check it out and see what's wrong."

"No!" Katie said. "I'm fine. I'll just—"

But Elliot Krieghoff wasn't taking no for an answer. He put his arm around her waist, hoisted her up, and settled her onto the seat of the snowmobile. "Don't be a dork, Metalface," he said. "You need somebody to take a look at it." He pointed at the sky. "It's starting to come down harder again. If that whiteout gets going again, you can't be wandering around in the snow with a broken ankle." He patted the seat. "Hop on, Chass."

I sat behind Katie. There was barely room for the three of us. Elliot gunned the machine, throwing up a huge plume of snow and tearing across the field. Onlookers had to scatter to get out of our way. I nearly fell off. Elliot laughed maniacally as we blasted across the field and out onto Broad Street.

"Wooooo!" Elliot yelled.

It didn't take us three minutes to reach Mrs. Krauthammer's place—though I was afraid we might die getting there. Elliot Krieghoff slammed us to a halt in the front yard, scooped Katie up, and carried her up onto the porch. I knocked on the door.

As Mrs. Krauthammer ushered us inside, Katie kept giving me this strange look.

Elliot Krieghoff set her down on the couch, then walked back outside. "I guess I'll hit the road," he called.

I followed him outside. "Hey, thanks," I said. "I don't think she could have made it this far in the snow."

"Whatever," he said. "No big thing."

Then he stopped and looked at me with a serious expression. "They say you saw who did it."

"Did what?"

"They say you saw who killed Miss Hill."

"Not really. I mean I saw somebody. But I didn't see their face."

Elliot Krieghoff kept staring at me. "You sure?"

I nodded.

He studied me intently. Then suddenly he jumped

on his snowmobile and tore away, spraying snow all over me.

I turned and went back into the house.

Katie lay on the couch, her face strained. I thought it was her ankle. But then she said to me, "He's the one."

"What?" I said.

"Elliot Kreighoff," she said. "He's the one I was talking about."

# FIFTEEN

**"REFRESH MY MEMORY,"** I said. "*What* one you were talking about, Katie?"

"I mean, I don't want to say it was definitely him . . ." Katie hobbled over behind me. "But Elliot's been Miss Hill's pet for years. And then I heard that lately they had some kind of big falling-out."

Mom's eyes blinked open. She looked over at me and gave me a wan smile.

"Hold on, Katie," I said. "Can I talk to Mom for a sec?"

"Sorry," Katie said.

"Hi," I said to Mom. "How you feeling?"

She nodded a little. "Hurts," she said.

"Do you know who shot you?" I said.

She shook her head. "I was just walking through the snow. Then someone called out, 'Hey, Chass.'"

"Chass?"

She touched her head gently. "Your hat. Remember I borrowed your hat? That goofy yellow hat with all the little strings hanging off it?"

"Oh," I said. "Yeah."

"It's a really distinctive hat. I'm sure they thought that I was you. Anyway, I turned around and *bam*. It felt like somebody had hit me in the shoulder with a crowbar. I didn't even see them. I just started running. They fired a couple more times. But in the whiteout I guess they lost me. Next thing I knew, I was walking up the stairs to the apartment."

"You should let her rest," Mrs. Krauthammer said.

I turned back to Mom. "Mom. Mom. Hey, Mom."

But Mom's eyes were closed. Her chest rose and fell slowly. She looked really peaceful. A lot more peaceful than usual. I could see lines around her eyes and at the corners of her mouth—lines I hadn't really noticed before. It made me a little sad to see them. She'd had a harder life than she deserved.

"Later," Mrs. Krauthammer whispered.

I turned back to Katie. "So. Elliot Krieghoff, huh?"

Katie shrugged. "I'm just saying . . ." Then she said, "I know who you ought to talk to . . ."

Lisa Lynn Rolweg was Elliot's girlfriend.

"*Former* girlfriend," she said as she met us at the door of her house. "*Ex*-girlfriend. *Totally-dumped-by-him-because-he's-a-douche-bag* girlfriend."

"Oh," I said.

"You want dirt on Elliot?" she said. "I totally have dirt on him. Come on in."

Lisa Lynn was a very pretty girl, in an ordinary bland Midwestern-girl way. I'm not trying to say that in a mean way. It's just that she was one of those people you could see at the mall or at the movies or on the street and you'd just pass by without thinking anything about her at all. She looked like a million other girls. Her hair was frosted blond; her makeup was just a teeny-weeny bit too strong for her features; and her clothes looked exactly like every other girl's clothes in

Greenville. Except mine and Katie's—and we don't really count because we're the town oddballs.

Lisa Lynn was hiding something, though. She wasn't a normal girl. I didn't know that, though, until I walked into her house.

It was a small house. But it felt even smaller because it was crammed to the rafters with stuff. Boxes and boxes and boxes of . . . well . . . stuff. You could hardly see the furniture in her living room for all the stuff. And where there weren't boxes of stuff, there were computers.

"I have an Internet business," she said, sweeping her hand around the room matter-of-factly. "I sell antique dolls."

A middle-aged woman was sitting amid all the boxes, crocheting. Her hair was in curlers and she wore a sweater with teddy bears appliquéd onto it. She looked up and smiled weakly at me. "Hello there," she said. Then she went back to crocheting.

"Like Barbies and stuff?" I said.

"Uh . . . *no*," Lisa Lynn said, as though I had asked an incredibly stupid question. "Dolls are dolls. Barbies are Barbies."

"Oh," I said. "Glad you cleared that up."

"I netted thirty-one thousand dollars last year."

"That's cool," I said.

"It *is* cool," she said. She hadn't smiled at me once. She sat down on one of the boxes. "So what do you want to know about Elliot?"

"You heard about Miss Hill, I assume?" I said.

She looked at me blankly. Apparently she was the only human being in the entire town of Greenville who didn't know Miss Hill had been murdered.

I told Lisa Lynn about what had happened.

The blood drained from her face. One of the computers made a *ping* noise. She went over and looked at the screen. "That lady in Thailand still hasn't got her Miss Huggable, Mom," she said irritably. "What's up with that?"

"I'll check, sweetie." Her mother set the crochet needle down and padded off down the hallway.

Lisa Lynn rolled her eyes. "Jeez Louise! I told her to ship that order like ten times!" She made a loud farting noise with her lips. "I swear to God I'm going to have to fire my own mother. How much does *that* suck?" Then she typed something rapidly into the computer. As she was typing she said to me, "You know, I would like to think I'm being paranoid or whatever? But Elliot and Miss Hill had something totally twisted going on.

He was always acting like they had some kind of big secret going. He'd always hint around about it. But then he'd never tell me anything. So if he killed her I wouldn't be even slightly shocked."

"Are you talking about, uh . . . an affair?" I said.

She turned and looked at me, her eyebrows shooting up. "Oh God, no! That's gross! She's like a million years old. No, it was something else."

"Like what?"

"That's the thing. I don't know."

"Well, can you guess?"

"Okay, first of all, it's not normal for a seventeen-year-old boy to talk about a teacher all the time. Or to go over to their house. But he was always like, 'Oh, Miss Hill this, Oh, Miss Hill, that, Miss Hill blah blah blah blah.' He was doing something musical over at her house. But I don't know what."

Elliot was the best trumpet player in the band. In fact, he was the best musician in the band. He was pretty much the golden boy of the school. He was one of two kids in contention for valedictorian, he lettered in three sports, he was president of the junior class, and he had the second-highest SAT score of anybody in Greenville High School.

"Well, what's so weird about that?" I said. "She had a lot of recording equipment. Maybe she was recording him playing trumpet or something."

Lisa Lynn gave me another look. "Why would he do that? He hates music."

I stared at her. "Then why's he in the band?"

"Because," she said in a slightly weary tone of voice, "Elliot has a thirty-year plan for his life. He calls it 'The Big Plan.' He's going to be valedictorian, president of this club, president of that club, then he's going to attend Princeton University. Then he's going to attend U of M Law. Then he's going to practice law in Greenville and run for fourth-district congressman. Then he's going to be governor. Then he's going to be president. In order to do all that crap, he has to be the best trumpet player, he has to be valedictorian, he has to be captain of all the sports teams that require the least work and athletic talent. Captain of the golf team. You think *that* takes talent?" She smiled a bitter little smile. "And, of course, he needs a better girlfriend than me."

"Oh," I said.

"Because—me?—I am too ordinary. I am too small town. I am too this, I am too that. So ka-ka-doody on me, sorry, see ya later." She waved bye-bye at me, then turned back and finished her e-mail.

"But you're not ordinary," I said. "You made thirty-one thousand dollars selling junk on eBay last year. Your own mother works for you."

She clickety-clacked for a while, then poked the enter button, stood up, and sighed loudly. "Everybody is who they are," she said. "I'm quoting Elliot there. He sat down with me a couple weeks ago and he said, 'Thirty years from now, you'll be a nice fat middle-aged Midwestern lady with curlers in her hair and a sweater with junk appliquéd on it. I can't be with somebody like that.'"

"He really said that?"

She shrugged. "I mean, he's probably right."

Lisa Lynn's mother came back into the room. "I called FedEx. Miss Huggable's hung up in customs outside Bangkok."

"Oh," Lisa Lynn said. "Figures." She typed another quick e-mail.

"So I heard that Miss Hill had a fight with Elliot recently."

"Yeah. Miss Hill was gonna give him a B in band."

"A B in band?"

"Yeah, he needs straight A's this year in order to be valedictorian. If he gets a B, Terri McGovern moves up to number one in the class. Then Elliot thinks he won't get into Princeton. If he doesn't get into Princeton, he won't become president and all his dreams will be shattered." Lisa Lynn said this in a flat, ironic way. Then she gave me a dry little smile. "See what I mean? That's how he thinks."

"And he got in a fight with Miss Hill over this?"

"Sure. He told her he'd kill her."

My eyes must have widened.

"I'm serious. I overheard the conversation. He was begging for extra credit and she told him she didn't do extra credit. So he told her his dad would, you know, sue her or something. And she just laughed at him. That was when he goes, 'You dried-up old biddy, I'm gonna slit your throat.'"

"Slit your throat. He didn't say he was going to shoot her."

"No. But if he really decided to kill her, he'd shoot her. He's kind of a mama's boy when you really get down to it. He'd be too chicken to use a knife."

"Well," I said. "That's good to know."

"Hey, I'm just telling it like it is," Lisa Lynn said.

"Does he have a gun?" I said.

Lisa Lynn frowned at me for a moment. "Where are you from?" she said.

"That's a longer story than you'd think," I said.

"Well, reason I ask, see, in Minnesota, everybody has a gun." She typed some more on her computer. The printer started humming away. "Elliot's dad has like . . . I want to say like fifty guns? Or sixty?"

"Okay."

"Big gun guy, Mr. Krieghoff. So, yeah, if Elliot wanted to shoot Miss Hill, it wouldn't be a problem."

I watched her work for a little while. She seemed to have almost forgotten I was there. I thought about everything she was saying. It all made sense. If Elliot killed Miss Hill and burned the school, no one would know that he'd made a B in band. It seemed like a lot of trouble to go to over a grade that wasn't even *that* bad. But then I guess I didn't want to be president of the United States. Maybe I'd have seen it differently if I did.

"You want a job, Chass?" Lisa Lynn said. "I need somebody reliable."

"Are you firing me, sweetie?" Lisa Lynn's mother said, looking up from her crocheting.

"You have to admit, you're not very good at the job," Lisa Lynn said to her mother. "Besides, the pay's not that great either. You could do better if you went back to working at the IGA."

Lisa Lynn's mother sighed loudly.

"See what I have to put up with?" Lisa Lynn said.

"I'll think about it," I said.

"Minimum wage plus a buck fifty an hour," Lisa Lynn said. She waggled her fingers in the air like she was typing. "E-mail me."

I stood up to go.

"Oh," Lisa Lynn said. "If you're really trying to find out whether he did it? He keeps a secret diary. If you can sneak into his room, it's under a loose board in the floor. He's so vain, he thinks that someday his diary will be, like, history. You know what I mean?"

"But if he thought it was going to be history," I said, "would he write, 'March twenty-sixth, killed my teacher'?"

"That," Lisa Lynn said, "is a really good question."

# SIXTEEN

**THE SNOW WAS** getting thick again when I reached Elliot Krieghoff's house. It was the biggest house in Greenville, a giant pile of stone that had probably been built about a hundred years ago. There was a stone fence around it and a huge front yard. As I went slogging up through the yard I started thinking about how weird it was that Elliot had swooped in on his snowmobile to pick Katie and me up after the fire. He wasn't in our class. And even if he had been, I couldn't see him giving either one of us the time of day.

Finally I reached the front door and rang the bell.

After a while Mr. Krieghoff answered. "Look," I said, "I just came to apologize for stealing the snowmobile. It really was kind of an emergency."

Mr. Krieghoff looked at me for a minute, then gave me an oily smile. "You want to come in, babe?"

A seventy-year-old dude who calls a high-school girl "babe." Nice, huh?

"Thanks," I said.

"I heard about your mom," he said. "Hey, I'm sorry . . ." He spread his hands. "I should have gone a little easier on you this morning."

"No, no," I said. "It's my fault. I got carried away."

He showed me his perfectly white dentures. "Not a problem. Water under the bridge. I'll have my body-shop guy take a look at it and you can just pay me for the damage. Shouldn't run more than two or three grand."

My eyes widened. "Two or three grand? It was already dented before I borrowed it."

Mr. Krieghoff laughed pleasantly. Or about as pleasantly as a guy like him can laugh. "That's a top-of-the-line model, though," he said, shrugging. "Has the graphics package and whatnot."

I stood there for a minute.

Mr. Krieghoff looked at his watch. "Anything else?"

"Is Elliot here?"

Mr. Krieghoff shrugged. "God only knows."

"Yeah," I said, "because I was supposed to pick up his notes from, uh, algebra class."

"Algebra?" Mr. Krieghoff scowled. "He's not in algebra."

"Two," I said. "Algebra Two."

"He's in calculus."

"That's what I mean," I said. "It starts with Algebra, uh, Two and then, you know, it goes on to . . . you know . . . calculus. The class does. That we're in. Together."

"Calculus."

"Calculus. Right."

Mr. Krieghoff stared at me for a minute. "Whatever," he said. "You know where his room is?"

"I'll find it."

He waved his hand in the direction of the stairs, and then walked away without saying another word. I headed for the stairs, glad to put some space between me and Mr. Krieghoff. For real, the guy gives me the creeps.

Like the rest of the house, Elliot's room looked as

clean and perfect as a four-star hotel. No junk on the shelves. No toys on the floor. No crumbs on the bed.

There was no art in the room. No posters of rock bands or sports stars on the wall, no duck-hunting prints, no nothing. The only decorations were trophies. And certificates. And pictures of Elliot with his dad. Elliot and his dad holding up a fish (a *prizewinning* fish, according to the certificate below the photo), photos of Elliot and his dad standing next to dead elk and deer and even some kind of African antelope. In every picture Mr. Krieghoff had this giant greasy grin and his hand was draped over Elliot's shoulder. And Elliot looked like he was having the worst time of his life. Trying to smile, but not really feeling it.

In a room as tidy as this, it didn't take two seconds to find the loose board, to pry it up and pull out the diary.

I opened it up and started reading at random.

JULY 18. Dad talked about THE BIG PLAN again. Every time I talk to him, it seems like he's added more junk to it. He's been reading all this stuff about Princeton, about where you're supposed to live and what you're supposed to major in and all the

stuff that will make you a WINNER, so that
when you graduate you'll be ON YOUR WAY
TO GREATNESS. I wish I had a different Dad.
I wish he was dead.

*Jeez!* I thought. *That's kinda depressing!* It didn't
quite jibe with all the golden-boy stuff.

AUGUST 21. Dad and I had another fight
today. He keeps telling me that Lisa Lynn is
not "worthy" of me, that she won't be
able to help me achieve all my goals and
objectives and stuff. God! I could kill him!

There were more like that. It sounded like this big
thirty-year plan that Lisa Lynn had told me about was
more Elliot's father's than it was Elliot's. I meant to
skip right to the end to see if he'd written anything
about killing Miss Hill. But then I saw something that
piqued my interest.

SEPTEMBER 9. Miss Hill sent me up to "the
place" again. It kinda freaks me out. I
guess I'll keep working for her. She's
promised to write me a really killer

recommendation to Princeton. That'll make Dad happy, anyway.

SEPTEMBER 12. Did another job for Miss Hill. The whole thing just totally creeps me out. I have to find out what's going on.

SEPTEMBER 19. I was working at Miss Hill's place the other night. She had to leave for a while. I got bored, so I started snooping around her house. Wow! Let me just say, this old lady is hiding some strange stuff. More later. I'm totally worn out.

SEPTEMBER 26. Another job for Miss Hill. I decided I had to find out what she was up to. My plan totally worked and I figured out her "big secret." What happened was, after the delivery I hid

And then, something strange happened. The next couple of pages were gone. I could see that maybe three or four pages had just been ripped right out of the diary. The next entry was a month later.

new girl at school. She's *hot*, too! Everybody was talking about her. Half the people are like, "oh, she's really cool" and half the people think she's weird or stuck-up. I can't decide. She doesn't dress like any of the girls or talk like any of the girls in Greenville. I would have liked to talk to her but she just seemed so...well, I don't know. So different, I guess. I didn't know what to say. I figured she might just think I was some jerky hick.

It took me a minute to realize he was talking about *me*!

JANUARY 21. I just keep thinking about HER. Lisa Lynn just seems so normal and boring now. All she can talk about is stupid eBay and how many dolls she's selling and what her net profit is and how many units and all this dumb crud. It's worse than talking to Dad. I think that SHE would not want to talk about dumb crud like that. I don't know exactly what she would talk about.

But it would be more interesting. I want to
ask her where she's from and what bands
she likes and all this stuff. But I just keep
not saying anything to her. She's only a
sophomore, so I don't have any classes
with her. I'd have to come up with some
kind of good excuse.

I don't know if you've ever read anybody else's diary
before . . . but it's a pretty weird experience. Especially
if they're writing about you. It made me feel a little icky
and dishonest. The more I read of the guy's diary, the
more sorry I was feeling for him. Plus, here he was getting all lathered up about me. And I hadn't even known
it! I read a couple more entries. He kept going on about
how great I looked and all this stuff. It was flattering.
But it also made me feel bad. So finally I flipped on
toward the end of the diary.

MARCH 19. Had a big fight with Miss Hill today
after school. She's giving me a B this
quarter. I got all mad at her. But the truth
is, I don't care. I only got mad because
I knew Dad would have a total fit. He'll
start going on about THE BIG PLAN, about

how I'm UNDERMINING him and how I'm so
FULL OF NEGATIVITY and all this crud.


MARCH 20. Dad said I have to go and beg
Miss Hill for extra credit. So I did. Miss Hill
told me there was no way. She told me
that my heart wasn't in the class and until
it was she wasn't going to reward me.
I said some terrible stuff to her. But as
soon as I got home, I called her up and
apologized. I said it was all because of my
dad. I said she could give me any grade
she wanted. I said I didn't care. She was
really nice and kind of got me calmed
down. I went over and we talked for a
long time. She told me I wasn't the only
person who'd been through stuff like this. I
think I'm going to break up with Lisa Lynn.
It'll make Dad happy. And me, too. I feel
like I haven't been honest with her. I don't
feel like I'm honest with anybody. What's up
with that?


MARCH 21. There's supposed to be a big
storm tomorrow. Maybe I can get a little

more snowmobiling in. When I'm on my snowmobile, I feel free. It's like the only time I feel that way. Maybe I'll go talk to HER. She lives in this cruddy apartment that Dad owns. (I'm sure Dad just rents it to them so he can perv on HER mom.) Anyway, I'm sure I could find some kind of excuse to get her to talk to me. I could pretend Dad sent me to fix something in their apartment or something dorky like that! I wonder if she would go on the snowmobile with me? Wooo-hoo!

And that was the last entry in the diary.

Nothing there about holding a grudge against Miss Hill. Nothing about wanting to burn down the school. It all sounded kind of hopeful.

Suddenly I heard a noise.

I looked up. And there was Elliot Krieghoff standing in the door staring at me. He blinked. Then he must have seen the board I'd pulled out of the floor, and the diary lying open in my lap.

His face flushed and a vein throbbed in his forehead. "What are you doing here?" he shouted. "That's my personal stuff!"

"I, uh—"

"That's mine!" He snatched the diary out of my hand. "Get out of here! Get out before I kill you!"

I jumped up like I'd been hit with a cattle prod. "Hey, whoa, hey, I'm sorry!" I said.

And I was. I was pretty sure he wasn't the killer. And now I'd gone in there and sponged up all his private feelings—including ones he had about me. It wasn't right.

"This is *mine*!" he said again. He was literally trembling now. "What are you even doing here?"

I didn't know what to say. Not even a clue. I just looked at the floor and edged toward the door. "I'm sorry," I said softly.

Now I mainly felt sorry for the guy. Here he was Mr. Hotshot, everybody looking up to him at school and everything—but inside, he didn't think much of himself. He felt like he was just a toy pushed around by his father.

I wanted to leave, to slink away from the room. But now he was standing between me and the door. So we just stood there

"How much did you read?" he said.

I'll be honest—I was tempted to lie. I was tempted to go with the old oh-I-just-barely-cracked-it-open-when-you-showed-up routine. But then he'd always wonder. I figured it was better to just tell him the truth.

I didn't actually have to open my mouth, though. I guess he saw it on my face.

"What gives you the right?" he said. "Those are my private thoughts." Then suddenly he looked like all the anger had evaporated. He flopped down on the bed and put his hands over his face. "God! You must think I'm a complete loser."

"No," I said. "It's kinda sweet really."

He looked up at me, then rolled his eyes and sighed.

"Who told you about it?" he said. "Lisa Lynn?"

I nodded.

He scowled. "She never understood me. She never really listened."

"Did you listen to her?"

He looked at me for a second, then suddenly he laughed a sort of sad, nervous laugh. "Yeah," he said. "You're right. I probably didn't. I suck at that."

"I was only here because . . . well, I thought maybe you'd killed Miss Hill. I was trying to find out."

He looked at me like I'd just gone crazy. "Miss Hill? What are you talking about?"

"They said you had a big argument with her. I figured . . ." I shrugged.

"You thought I'd *kill* her? Over some stupid grade that I'd be able to pull up by the end of the year anyway? What do you think I am—some kind of monster?"

"Sorry," I said. "But somebody did it. I'm just trying to find out who."

At school Elliot always seemed like this invincible guy, like he walked around inside this force field of charisma. But now he seemed deflated and pitiful.

"Why?" he said. "Why do you even care who did it?"

I sat there and thought about it for a minute. I didn't know the guy at all, didn't know if I could trust him. But like I was saying earlier, I've just gotten tired of lying to everybody.

"Long story," I said. And I suppose I could have left it at that. But I didn't. I told him everything. Well, not *everything*! That would have taken all day. But I told him enough.

When I was done, he narrowed his eyes and looked at me for a long time, like he was trying to figure out why I would tell such an elaborate lie. "Okay, good story," he said. "But total bull."

I just looked at him. I guess I really didn't care if he believed me or not.

He stared at me for a while. Finally he said, "You're *serious.*"

I nodded.

Then he said, "Okay, well, check this out. There *is* a connection. Between Miss Hill and that Van Epps guy."

"Yeah? What is it?"

"Well . . . it has to do with this job I had for Miss Hill."

"What was the job?"

"Well, it had to do with recording stuff."

This didn't sound like all the mysterious stuff he was alluding to in the diary. "So you were, what, an engineer or something?"

He laughed. "Not even close. It was more like . . . I was a driver."

I frowned, trying to figure out what he was talking about.

"I don't know if you knew," he said. "But Miss Hill doesn't drive."

"For real?"

"Yeah. She has some kind of weird phobia. So wherever she goes, it's always in a cab. But she does own a . . . vehicle."

I cocked my head. The way he said it, it sounded like it wasn't a normal car.

"She keeps it in her garage. On the outside, it looks like a normal van. But inside . . . well, it's not normal."

"What do you mean?"

He waved his hand like he'd started telling the story in the wrong place. "Never mind. You'll get the picture in a minute."

I shrugged.

"Okay," he said, "so here's how it worked. Every couple of weeks Miss Hill would call and she'd say, 'Okay, we're doing it tonight.' She never said what. Just 'it.' We're doing 'it.' So on those nights, I'd drive to her house, go into her garage and get into the van. And once I was in the van, she'd open the garage door. Then I'd leave. I'd drive up to this place called the Forest Glen Clinic."

"What is it? Some kind of hospital?"

He smiled thinly. "You could say that. It's a loony bin out in the country north of Brainerd. It's like this really creepy, high-security place."

"You mean like a prison?"

"Not exactly. It's a private facility. Say, like if you're a rich person. And you've got a son who's like some kind of total sociopath psycho monster. And he did something really really bad. Maybe killed somebody? Sometimes, instead of trying the case, the state will let you plead insanity. In which case, you go to a loony bin instead of prison. If you're rich enough, the state will say, okay, instead of going to the state psycho ward, you can save the taxpayers some bucks and stick them in Forest Glen."

"Whoa!" I said. "Creepy."

"No kidding. And this place, dude, it's like right out of a horror movie! You drive up and there's this huge stone wall. There's no sign or anything. You stop at the gate and a guy with a clipboard comes out and says, 'Hello, sir.' You tell him your name and he's like, 'Step out of the car, sir.' You get a pat-down search. Then they scan your car with all kinds of gizmos. Then they give you an ID card to clip on your shirt. And they're like, 'We can track you at all times with this card, sir. Don't lose the card. Or we can't be responsible for what happens to you.'"

"Whoa!"

"I'm telling you. And then you drive in, and after the wall, there's a giant fence covered with razor wire. And there's guard towers. And there's dudes with rifles up there. I mean it's like supermax prison. Shoot to kill, you know?"

"So what's this have to do with Miss Hill?"

"I'm getting there." He sat down on the bed next to me. I could smell him, the smell of his shaving cream or his deodorant or something. I wasn't sure if I liked it. "Anyway, so then there's this big mansion-type building in the middle of this wide-open lawn. Must be like a hundred years old. Turrets and bars over the windows and stuff. It's the insane asylum out of some horror flick.

"So I back the van up at this loading dock around the back side of the building. I leave the van. Then there's more guards and more forms to fill out and stuff. And they take me in to see the director of the place. He's all business, you know. Like a cop? No sense of humor. He has me sign this form. Then he says, 'Return to the vehicle, Mr. Krieghoff.' Everybody calls me Mr. Krieghoff. Which is very weird, you know?

"So then I go back and sit in the van, with the rear end pulled up to the loading dock. The way I'm sitting I can't see what they're loading into the van. I've got the engine running. Then there's some thumping and bumping. Then this huge dude in a white coat comes out and says, 'You can go, Mr. Krieghoff.' So I drive back to Miss Hill's place. The garage door opens. I back the van in. The door comes down."

"So what's in the back of the van?" I said.

"What? You mean *who's* in the back of the van?"

"Oh," I said, flushing. "Okay, yeah, duh."

"That's the thing!" Elliot leaned toward me, eyes widening. "See, I can't see in the back of the van. It's like it's walled off from the cab of the van. The back part, it's got this kind of . . . cage. It's welded inside the van. Solid steel plate. The doors in the back of the van are the same thing. Solid steel."

"So okay . . . who's in there?"

"Here's where it starts to get weird. Once I've parked the van, Miss Hill tells me to go back inside the house and watch TV. So I leave her there in the garage with the van. Then I hear more thumping and bumping . . ."

"And?" I said.

Elliot raised his hands in front of him. "And . . . nothing. Well, not *nothing* nothing. I mean all that happens after that is you hear music coming out of the back of the house. She's got a studio back there. And it's basically . . . you know, it sounds like it's a recording session. It's hard to tell, though. The room's soundproofed, so you can't really hear much. Just the bass. Or when the door's open now and then, you can hear some music playing."

I squinted at him. "That's *it*?"

"That's it."

"Then what?"

"The recording session lasts a long time. Sometimes all night. So I usually just fall asleep on the couch. Eventually Miss Hill wakes me up. She'll say something like, 'He's ready.'"

"He," I said. "She says 'he.'"

"*He's* ready." Elliot looked out the window at the snow. "Then I go back, get in the van, drive back to the loony bin, and we do everything we did before. Except backward. I back up to the loading dock, thumpety-thumpety-thumpety. Then I go to the director and sign forms. Then I come home and go to sleep."

"You do this on school days?"

"Never. Friday or Saturday nights only."

"So you've never seen this guy?" I said. "You don't know who's back there?"

Elliot gave me a sneaky smile. "I didn't say that."

I punched his arm. "Dude! Give it up! Who's the guy in the van?"

"One time I parked so that I could kinda see into the loading-dock area." He leaned toward me. "There were these two guards in white coats. And they had this guy on a dolly, like Hannibal Lecter? He was in a straitjacket. And then his arms and legs were locked to the dolly with steel straps. And he wore this creepy iron mask so he couldn't chew your face off!"

"Whoa! Are you serious?"

Elliot Krieghoff laughed. "No. I'm kidding. Actually, what happened was, after I left Miss Hill in the garage with the van, I hid in the bathroom in the back hallway of her house. With the door cracked a little. So I could see out? After a couple minutes the door to the garage opens and Miss Hill wheels this guy out in a wheelchair. And I mean, talk about the unscariest guy you've ever seen in your life. Well, creepy. But not scary—if you see the difference."

"I'm not sure I do."

"The dude in the wheelchair . . . he's this little dwarfy-type guy. He's wearing big weird-looking sunglasses. And his legs are kinda shriveled up. And one of his arms is tiny." He held out his hands about six or eight inches apart. "Like . . . bigger than G.I. Joe? But smaller than a normal baby's arm."

My eyes widened. "Holy crap!" I said. "It's Kyle Van Epps's brother!"

Elliot nodded, his eyes glistening. "Yeah, dude! The insane wack-job lunatic killer in the van is Kyle Van Epps's brother."

"You know the story?" I said. "About Kyle Van Epps's family?"

"C'mon. Everybody in Greenville knows that story." He smiled. "But only a few people—me being one of them—know about Cale."

"Cale?"

"That's his name, Chass! Cale. Cale Van Epps."

"Oh," I said.

I don't know why, but suddenly I shivered.

"So do you think *he's* the one that killed their father back in the day? I mean everybody thinks it was Kyle. But if it was . . . then how come Cale is the one in the high-security crazy house?"

Elliot shrugged. "Exactly! The story you hear around town is that Kyle was the one who did it for sure. But if that's true, how come Cale's the one in the loony bin? And why doesn't anybody know about that part of the story? I mean, I've asked a bunch of people. And none of them know anything about what happened to Cale."

"So you've told people what you do for Miss Hill?"

He shook his head. "No. That was part of the job requirement. Total secrecy. Total. When she first offered me the job, she said that if I do the job perfectly,

I'll get the best recommendation in the world. It'll get me into any college on the planet. But it's conditional. If I breathe a word—a *word!*—to anybody ... *boom,* that's it, game over. No recommendation." He raised one eyebrow. "Oh, and by the way, the pay's good, too. Two hundred bucks each session." He grinned. "Plus ... two hundred more goes in the bank. If you don't tell anybody, when you graduate, you get the whole pile that was stuck in the bank." He lowered his voice. "Chass, I've got five grand sitting in the bank right now!"

We sat there silently for a while.

Suddenly he turned away from me sharply and started wiping at his eyes.

"Man, it's not right!" His voice broke and his shoulders started trembling. I could see then that he'd been putting up a front all day, like what happened to Miss Hill wasn't bothering him. "She was a good lady! Who would do a thing like this?"

"I don't know," I said. "That's what I'm trying to find out."

It took Elliot a little while to calm down. Finally he turned to me, his eyes rimmed with red, and said, "You must think I'm a complete loser."

"What, because you feel sad about somebody getting murdered?"

He stood up, blew his nose, and threw the tissue in the trash. Then he put the diary back underneath the floorboard and closed it up.

"So what do you think it's all about?" I said finally. "Why did Kyle's brother come to Miss Hill's house?"

"I guess he recorded songs there."

"Yeah, but why? Why there? If he's really a psycho killer, why are they letting him out to make music?"

"I guess . . . Kyle Van Epps must have pulled some strings."

"Yeah, but I still just don't see why. Was this guy some musical genius? I mean he spent the first twenty years of his life locked inside a grain silo."

"Beats me. Maybe he just likes music. Maybe Kyle felt bad about him being in the loony bin and wants him to be able to do something he enjoys."

"So did he sing? Did he record songs? Did he write songs? What was the deal?"

"Well . . . I did find some stuff one day. I was trying to figure out what her big secret was. See what this means to you." Elliot went over to his desk and rummaged around in a drawer. Finally he found some papers. He handed them to me. "Here."

I looked at the paper on top. It was musical notation paper with music and words scrawled on it in pencil.

Something about it seemed vaguely familiar. Then it hit me. It was a song that had been recorded a couple years back by some girl pop star. I couldn't remember who she was, but the song was right there in my memory. It was one of those songs that you heard everywhere you went for about three months. And then it was gone.

I flipped to the last page of the paper. At the bottom it said *copyright C. Van Epps.*

I felt my eyes widen. "Can I use your computer?"

Elliot shrugged. "Sure."

I jumped in the chair in front of his computer, logged on to BMI, one of the companies that collects royalties for songwriters. I searched the site for Cale Van Epps. A list of songs popped up: 1,729 of them.

"Oh my God!" I said.

I took one of the songs at random, ran it through a search engine. Nothing. I tried another. The second song came up on a list of Billboard Top 100 Country Hits. It had peaked at number forty-seven for a singer named Jim Ed Brown in 1968. I ran searches on more songs. Most of them went nowhere. But not all of them. I found a pop hit by an Australian singer in 1993, a couple of country hits ranging from 1971 to 2004. I even found an R&B hit from last year. All written by Cale Van Epps. I couldn't believe it.

"That little dude is a machine!" Elliot said. "He's probably written, like, dozens of hits."

"Uh . . . no," I said. "Based on how many I've looked at? If you do the math? Probably more like hundreds."

Elliot gawked at me.

"Well," I said, "now we know where Miss Hill's money was coming from."

"What do you mean?"

"Here's the thing that most people don't know about the music business. All the money's in songwriting."

"What do you mean?"

"All those pretty girls that you see shaking their booties on MTV and all those rappers with the washboard abs and the purple cars with giant chrome wheels? Those guys make nothing."

"Really?"

"Totally. The real money's made by all these guys you never see. Songwriters. They make about a penny every time a CD gets pressed, half a cent every time it gets downloaded on iTunes, a couple nickels every time it plays on the radio. Which sounds like nothing. But after a while it adds up."

"Huh," Elliot said.

"Now think about this. If you've written, say, a hundred hit songs? And those songs keep getting played on oldies stations and stuff? And people keep down-loading them? And maybe sometimes somebody puts one in the background of an advertisement or a movie? Hey, you could be looking at thousands and thousands of bucks rolling in every month. And you don't have to lift a finger. It just rolls in. And that's not counting the money you get while a song's hot. One huge song could be worth like three, four, five hundred grand in one year!"

Elliot shrugged. He seemed to be losing interest.

"You know what they say in the FBI?" I said. "The way to solve crimes?"

Elliot shrugged again.

"Follow the money."

Elliot frowned. He just didn't seem to get why I was getting excited.

"Come on!" I said. "Let's say Cale's written a hundred songs that actually became hits. Let's say each song's worth a hundred grand over the years. That's probably conservative. That's ten million bucks! Where did the money go?"

"Are you saying somebody stole his money? Like maybe his brother?"

"I don't know. But it's an interesting question, don't

you think? I mean, a lot of people would kill for ten million bucks."

"Okay . . ."

"I mean, think about it. Why all the big secrecy? If everything's cool, if everything's straight, if everything's honest—why did Miss Hill have to swear you to secrecy just because some guy is recording songs at her house?"

"I don't know."

"Me neither," I said. "But I'm gonna find out."

# SEVENTEEN

**TEN MINUTES LATER** I was back at Miss Hill's house. The snow was coming down harder again. I could still see a little, but it was definitely heading in the direction of whiteout again. Still, I had no problem seeing the yellow crime-scene tape stretched across the door.

For a moment I hesitated about trying to go through the tape. But I figured, hey, somebody already trashed the place looking for something. What could I do to make it worse. Right?

I wasn't sure exactly what I was looking for. But I had a better idea now than I did when Katie and I went in a few hours ago.

Nothing had changed inside the house. Same cool furniture, same expensive-looking art on the walls.

But I realized I hadn't checked out the entire house yet. Was there a basement? An attic? I wasn't sure. And I hadn't been in the garage either.

As it turned out, the garage didn't tell me much. It was full of the usual junk you find in garages—rakes and shovels and snowblowers. But that was about it.

The basement was a different story. I realized I was onto something as soon as I opened the door. It wasn't the sort of normal junky door you'd put on your basement. It was a heavy steel door with a honking big bolt lock on it and hinges that looked like they'd hold up to a battering from the Incredible Hulk.

You didn't put a door like that on something . . . unless you were seriously trying to keep people out. Which meant there was something valuable there, right? You don't lock dime-store jewelry in a safe.

I opened the massive door, flipped on the light, and walked down. Miss Hill's basement looked like the interior of an office building. White walls, very bright fluorescent lights, a ceiling made from rectangular acoustical tiles. No windows, no doors. In one corner was a desk with a computer on it. And all the way around the rest of the room were filing cabinets. Dozens and dozens of them. I felt pretty sure the filing cabinets didn't have schoolwork in them. I mean, there wasn't much paperwork in band class anyway.

I pulled one open at random. The cabinet was full of papers with numbers on them. It was some kind of financial stuff. I don't know diddly about financial stuff—so it meant nothing to me.

I put it back, looked in another filing cabinet. This was a royalty statement from BMI. It showed that a song called "End of the Dream" had made thirty-six cents in royalties during the first quarter of 1974. I looked more closely. File folder after file folder, each one with the name of a song.

So here it was, records of how much money Cale Van Epps had made writing songs. I already had guessed that he'd made a ton of money. So beyond that, I wasn't superinterested. But I kept checking. Follow the money, right? If Miss Hill had been killed over money, this probably told the story of why. I kept opening filing-cabinet drawers and finding stuff that didn't seem very important to me.

Then I saw one that was intriguing. It said *Apex Media* on the front. Apex was the name of Kyle Van Epps's company. I pulled it open, took out the first file. It was really old and crumbly. Inside were a bunch of legal documents. The top document said *Will and Trust of Opal Van Epps*. The next one said *Trust and Indenture of Cale Van Epps*. The next file said *Incorporation Documents—Apex Records*.

I'll tell you, my eyes were starting to glaze over. I mean, I was sure this stuff meant something. But what? All this legal junk meant nothing to me.

I realized that I had a big problem here. Mom had been trying to dig up dirt about Kyle Van Epps my whole life. And this was probably the mother lode. I could tell from how old and crumbly all these papers were that I'd found stuff about the founding of the little record company that Kyle Van Epps had eventually turned into a huge global media business.

I realized I needed Mom's advice. Big-time. The phones hadn't been working on Broad Street because the falling cell tower had torn down the lines. But that didn't mean all the phones in Greenville were dead.

I picked up the phone on the desk. Thankfully, it worked fine. I checked the phone book and dialed Mrs.

Krauthammer's house. She answered immediately and I asked if Mom was in any condition to talk on the phone.

A few seconds later I heard her voice. Weak, but clear. "Hi, sweetie."

"Hey, Mom!" I can't tell you how relieved I was. "Thank goodness. How you doing?"

"Feeling a little rough," she said.

"I bet." I paused. "Look, I'm over at Miss Hill's house. I've found all this stuff in her basement. Stuff that's related to Kyle Van Epps." I gave her a quick outline of everything that Elliot had told me about Cale Van Epps. Then I told her what I'd found in the basement of Miss Hill's house.

"You are *kidding*!" she said. "My gosh, Chass, this may be what I've been searching for all these years!"

A rush of excitement ran through me. The notion that we might be on the verge of finally figuring this thing out—well, I can't even tell you how strong the feeling was. It was like this big fountain of relief and happiness.

"What do I need to find out?"

"Pull out the documents you just told me about," she said. "The will and the other stuff."

"Okay," I said. I pulled out the will first, started

reading it out loud to Mom. I wasn't really paying attention to what it said. It just sounded like legal mumbo jumbo to me. Finally I noticed that I hadn't heard anything from Mom.

"Mom?" I said. "You there?"

There was a long pause. Finally Mom said, "Are you aware of what that just said?"

"Uh . . ." I said. Which is my extremely articulate and clever way of saying *No clue!*

"What it says is that Kyle Van Epps didn't inherit anything from his mom. Every last penny she owned went to Cale."

"So?" I said.

"Read that other thing. The one that says *Trust and Indenture.*"

I did what she said. It was like a thirty-page document. Talk about boring! It was gibberish to me. I read for a long time. Finally Mom cut me off. "See if there's something that says *Involuntary Commitment Order,* or something like that."

I had to dig around, but I found it. I paid a little more attention to this one as I read it to her. It basically said that a court had decided back in 1967 that Cale Van Epps was "developmentally disabled" and should be sent to the funny farm. It didn't say anything about him being charged with a crime. I was surprised to see the name on the bottom of the document. There was a line for the lawyer who filed the papers to the court. It was a name I recognized. Elliot Krieghoff.

Of course, then I realized it wasn't the Elliot Krieghoff that I knew. The date next to the name was from 1967. Elliot wasn't even born until like several decades later. Still, it was kind of an odd coincidence.

Mom interrupted my thoughts. "Okay, now read me the incorporation documents for Apex Records."

I started reading. It was more boring legal mumbo jumbo that I couldn't make any sense of.

Finally she stopped me. "Wow," she said. "Wow. That's all I have to say. Wow."

There was a long, long silence. I had no idea what was such a big deal about this stuff.

As I was sitting there, something came back to me. The label on Kyle Van Epps's record "My Confession." Underneath the song title was the name of the songwriter, C. Van Epps. At the time I'd thought it was a misprint, that it was supposed to be *K*. Van Epps. But now I knew better. The song had been written by *Cale* Van Epps.

Which meant that Mom had been digging in the wrong place. Kyle slept in the house. But *Cale* slept in—

Suddenly the hair stood up on the back of my neck. Why? For a second I wasn't sure. And then I realized. I'd heard a noise somewhere. I couldn't quite put my finger on what it was. A squeak? A soft crunch? Something like that. It was as though someone was upstairs in Miss Hill's house. Someone who was walking very, very, very stealthily.

"Mom," I said.

"You realize what this means?"

"Mom? I just realized something—"

"Everyone has always thought that Kyle Van Epps inherited his father's farm after his mother died. And that he sold it. They thought that he bought Apex Records with his own money. And then he built it into this huge fortune. Do you realize what this means?"

"Look, Mom—"

"Chass, this is huge. It means that Kyle Van Epps doesn't really own his company. The real owner of Apex Global Media is Cale! Not Kyle!"

"Mom," I said, "we've gotten everything backward."

I heard another squeak from the floorboards above me. Somebody was *definitely* up there.

I tried to tell myself that maybe it was just Chief Norgren. But if it was? Why was he creeping around like that? No, it had to be somebody else. Chief Norgren would be marching around making a ton of noise. Then I put it all together. There had been something that was puzzling me all day. There had been footsteps up to the door of Miss Hill's house when Katie and I broke in. But no footprints coming out. We must have interrupted whoever had broken into the house as they were tearing up Miss Hill's music studio. So they must have fled out the back door when they heard us trying to get in. So whatever they were looking for, they hadn't found it. And now they were back.

The question was, did they know I was here?

There was a slight click on the line as I was trying to figure out what to do.

"Exactly!" Mom said. "We've got everything backward."

"No, it's not that," I whispered. I was trying to keep my voice down so that whoever was upstairs couldn't hear me. "It's Cale. Not Kyle. Kyle's brother *Cale* wrote the song. So the clue about the murder is in the *silo*! Not in the house!"

"Oh my God!" Mom said. "You're right. It's in the silo!"

I whispered again, this time even more softly. "Mom! Mom! I think there may be somebody upstairs."

Then I heard something on the line—an intake of breath. And somehow I knew it wasn't Mom.

Too late I realized what the click I'd just heard was. Somebody had picked up the phone upstairs and was listening in on the line.

"This is huge," Mom said. "We've got him! The silo! It's just a matter of—"

"Mom," I said. "I have to go."

"Look, honey, if you get a chance, I want—"

There was another click. Then silence. Whoever was upstairs must have cut the phone line. I felt a twist of dread in my gut.

Then there were loud footsteps. Running. Whoever it was, they were coming for me. I looked around trying to find some kind of weapon. A silver-handled letter opener lay on the desk. I grabbed it, held it like an ice pick, and ran to the foot of the stairs.

The footsteps beat me to the door that came down from upstairs. I steeled myself, ready to fight to the death against whatever monster threw open the door.

Strangely, though, the door didn't open. There was only one sound. The sound of the door being locked. Then the footsteps moved away from the door. I heard some soft thumping and bumping, then something that sounded like water sloshing.

After that I heard footsteps moving briskly across the floor. A door slammed. And then . . . nothing.

I realized I must have scared them off again. But whoever it was, I realized that he probably would have interpreted what Mom said on the phone to mean that we knew who the killer was. So maybe he had decided that his first order of business was to find Mom and silence her for good.

I ran up the stairs and turned the handle of the door. It didn't budge. Whoever it was, he'd definitely locked the door. The heavy . . . massive . . . humongous . . . solid freakin' steel door.

I pounded on it with my fist. But I might as well have been pounding on a thirty-ton boulder. It wasn't moving.

The good news was that the killer wasn't coming after me. The bad news was that I was stuck there for a while. Maybe until he came back. But in this weather, that could be a while.

*Okay,* I thought, *this isn't so bad, right? All I have to do is take my time, be smart, figure a way out.*

I felt a lot better. The killer wasn't so bright after all. There had to be a dozen ways to get out of here. Maybe I could use the knife to cut a hole in the floor.

Then I smelled something and realized I'd under-estimated him a little.

Smoke. A tiny curl of it coming from under the bot-tom of the door.

*Oh*, I thought. *I get it. We're on fire.*

# EIGHTEEN

IT'S FUNNY THE things that go through your mind when you find out you're about to burn to death.

When I was in the school and it was on fire ... I don't know, I felt scared. But I didn't feel like I was about to die. I mean there are windows in pretty much every room in the school. Worst-case scenario, we always had the option of bailing out through a window. Maybe you'd get banged up when you landed or whatever. But I never actually thought, *Hey, I'm gonna die!*

But now I was in a different situation. No windows, no doors (except the steel door at the top of the stairs), no working phone, no radio, no Internet . . .

You'd think I would have been totally frantic and freaking out. But I wasn't. I just felt this gloomy calm come over me. I clumped back down the stairs and walked around the basement, looking at things. Hanging on the wall over the desk was Miss Hill's college diploma. She had majored in music and minored in accounting.

*Huh,* I thought. *Now there's a weird combination.*

On the floor next to the desk was a big pile of cola cans. I noticed that Miss Hill bought store-brand cola. I wondered idly why somebody who obviously had a fair amount of money would get all cheap when it came to cola.

I kept wandering around the room. Finally I pulled out some files and looked at the royalty statements for various songs. Cale Van Epps had written a song in 1971 called "She's So Mysterious" that had been recorded by the Monkees. He still got royalties off it, thirtysomething years later. It hadn't been a hit or anything. But every time some nostalgia junkies bought a Monkees CD, good old Cale got paid. Turned out he'd made a hundred and four thousand bucks on that song. Not even a hit. Sweet!

And then I started wondering, how does a guy who's smart enough to write zillions of hit songs get declared incompetent and get shoved in a loony bin for the rest of his life?

It was an interesting question. I pulled open another drawer, expecting more royalty statements. But instead I found more of the boring accounting junk. I looked at the top of the page. It read, STATEMENT OF ACCOUNTS, GREENVILLE HIGH SCHOOL.

I put it back, closed the drawer.

There was a definite smell of smoke in the room. But there wasn't so much that you had any problem breathing. Other than a few wisps coming under the door, you couldn't even see it. If I hadn't known better, I wouldn't have guessed that the building above me would probably soon collapse and kill me.

No doors, no windows, no phone, no radio, no Internet, no . . .

*Wait a minute!* I thought. I didn't know that there was no Internet. The killer had cut the phone line. But the Internet probably went through something else.

I wiggled the mouse, bringing Miss Hill's computer to life. She was already logged on to the Internet.

I logged on to MySpace and tried IMing everybody

I could think of. Nobody was logged on. Then I thought . . . *What about Elliot?*

As it turned out, Elliot *was* online! So I typed

Hey, it's Chass. I'm in Miss Hill's house. It's
burning down and I can't get out.

**LOL!**

Dude, Im serious.

**Well, get out!!!!!!!!**

Can't. Trapped.

**How?**

Basement. Steel door. No windows no doors.

**Call 911.**

No phone.

**I'll call.**

Too slow. Roads bad. Only have 2 or 3 minutes.

Please think of something.

You know, it's kinda pathetic, but there are some things where I just feel like, *Well, a boy could figure this out better than me.* I mean, it's dumb, but, like, girls are mostly hopeless when it comes to stuff like how do guns work or how do you soup up a car or whatever. And I just felt like a boy would have a better idea about how to get out of a burning building than I would.

Elliot's response was quick.

**Go through the wall, Chass.**
Huh?
**Go kick the crap out of the wall. Might just be drywall. Breaks easy.**

I did what he said. I yanked over one of the filing cabinets, stomped the wall. Big mistake. It felt like I'd stomped a boulder. Behind the drywall, there was nothing but solid concrete block. I tried kicking holes in the wall in several other places. Same thing all the way around the basement.

Didn't work, *I typed*. Solid concrete.
**What about the stairwell?**
What about it?
**Basement walls concrete. Not main floor.**

I hadn't even thought of that. I ran over and climbed the stairs. I could feel heat radiating through the door. The paint was actually blistering and peeling off the inside of the door. I braced myself against one side of the stairwell and kicked the wall with all my might.

It turned out to be overkill. The wall was so eaten up by the fire that it was like kicking paper. Flames poured through the hole. I jerked my foot back. Through the hole I could see nothing but fire. I ran back down the stairs.

Thanks, *I typed*. I think that'll work.
**Just get out!!!!!!**

Then something struck me. The name I'd seen on that document. Elliot Krieghoff. Could it have been his dad? I realized I didn't know what Mr. Krieghoff's first name was. Mr. Krieghoff was pretty old to have a son as young as Elliot. He might have been old enough that he could have been practicing law here in Greenville back in the sixties.

*I typed:* Was your dad a lawyer once?
**Dude, get out!!!!!!!!!!!!!!!**

*What was I thinking?* Elliot was right. Now was not the time to be farting around on the computer. Then I started opening up Miss Hill's el cheapo cola and pouring it on my head. I figured my only hope at this point was to just blast through the house and hope I could get out without getting burned to death. And if I was going to be successful at that, the best thing I could do would be to get my clothes all wet.

Four cans of cheap cola later, I was covered in foam and soaking wet. I took a sip of the cola. *Not bad!* I thought. I've always liked real Coke best. But this stuff was pretty good.

I opened two more cans, then charged up the stairs. The fire had burned right through the wall where I'd kicked it. I couldn't see anything but fire on the other sides of the bare two-by-fours in the wall. Even the wooden two-by-fours were burning.

I covered my skin with my shirt, pulled my hood over my face, and pulled the drawstring as tight as I could. Then I charged into the room spraying cola all over the place. Everything was burning. Everything. The heat was so intense . . . I was going to say it was like walking into an oven. But actually I bet it was a lot hotter.

Smoke obscured everything.

I screamed. It was the most horrible feeling I'd ever had in my life. I just started running around wildly, spraying cola all over the place. Not that it did any good.

I was sure I was going to die.

And then I saw light. A window. I threw myself at the light. There was a giant crash.

And then I was lying in the snow, burning.

I rolled over and over and over, trying to put out the fire. When the cheerleaders had said I was on fire over at the high school, they were kind of overstating the case. There'd been some smoke, maybe a tiny bit of flame. But this time, no joke, I was totally on fire.

I rolled and rolled and rolled until I was sure I wasn't burning anymore.

And then suddenly I was lying on my back in the middle of the same gray, swirling nothingness that I'd been in and out of all day.

I couldn't see the fire. I couldn't see the sun or the trees or the sky or the bushes or the road. Just the snow. I was freezing cold. Snowflakes were falling on my face. Each one, as it hit the parboiled skin of my face, felt like a tiny torch.

*Well,* I thought, *I'm alive anyway. Which is cool.*

And then I heard footsteps behind me. I looked up expecting to see a person appearing out of the snow. But it wasn't a person.

It was a wolf.

Hackles raised. Teeth bared. Cold blue eyes pinned on my face. For a moment we just looked at each other.

Then the wolf began creeping toward me.

"Oh for godsake," I said. "Eaten by wolves. This is all I need."

# NINETEEN

**WE'RE IN AMERICA.** I mean, maybe there are places in the world where you have to be worried about being eaten alive by wolves. Transylvania or Moldavia or someplace. I mean, anyplace that ends with *-ania* or *-avia* or *-stan*, you could probably get eaten by wolves. But in *America*?

Look. Run over by a school bus? Drowned while waterskiing? Electrocuted in a tanning bed? Choked to death on an olive pit? Maybe even skinned and eaten by a serial killer with freaky teeth? Okay, sure—that stuff could happen in America. But eaten by *wolves*? Dude! Come on!

I guess it sort of ticked me off. I jumped up and jabbed my finger at the wolf. "Hey! What do you think you're doing, you stupid wolf? You're supposed to be afraid of me! It's people like me that make animals like you extinct, you stupid dumb moron!"

This speech really seemed to impress the wolf.

It didn't even blink. It just eased forward about half a step, still growling, still baring its teeth. It was skinny and its ribs were sticking out. I guess it was hungry enough that even *I* looked tasty.

So it opened its jaws and leaped at me.

I put up my hands to try to fight off the wolf.

Next thing I knew, there was a huge thump and an impact that threw me into the snow. It took me a second to recover my wits. When I did, I found the wolf lying on my chest.

I shoved it as hard as I could, expecting it to make a grab for my throat with its razor-sharp teeth. But instead the wolf was limp as a noodle. It just sort of slid over sideways and lolled on the snow like it was sleeping.

That was when I noticed that the ground around

me was littered with debris. The snow had gone black. Two-by-fours, smoldering bits of paper, a corkscrew, a coat hanger, melted pieces of plastic. Junk everywhere. And then I figured it out. Something inside Miss Hill's house had exploded. A propane tank, a gas can, a nuclear bomb—I don't know. But whatever it was, it had tossed junk all over the place. And apparently something flung from the house had smacked the wolf in the head.

I poked the wolf with my toe. It opened one eye and peered at me.

I decided it was time to put as much distance between me and that wolf as possible. Also between me and the burning house. I couldn't see Miss Hill's house. But I could hear it. The fire made a throaty roar, like a bonfire on steroids. Maybe she had two propane tanks in there. Or two gas cans. Or two nuclear bombs. Whatever. Point is, I didn't want to be there if and when something else decided to blow up.

I stood up and staggered into the snow, heading in the opposite direction from the house. The falling snow was so thick again that I couldn't see where I was going. Once again, I was back to Snow World.

I was feeling a little stunned. But not so stunned that I didn't notice the following fact: being soaked with store-brand cola is not comfortable in fifteen-degree weather.

And my coat wasn't doing much to cut the wind now either. You probably didn't know that parkas come in regular and extra crispy. But they do. If you don't believe me, put on your parka and walk through a burning building. What went in as a nice puffy, soft coat that keeps you warm in the winter comes out as this thin, crackly, smelly shell that does very little to help you stay warm. I realized I needed to clean up and get warm clothes on.

I also knew that the killer knew Mom was alive. And he was going to find her. In a town like this, where everybody seemed to know everything about everybody, it was a sure bet that he'd figure out where Mom was. I decided to head back to Mrs. Krauthammer's place.

It probably didn't take me more than a minute to find a landmark. But it seemed like hours. Finally I bumped into a street sign. I was on the right track.

After that, things didn't go so easily. I kept getting turned around and going in the wrong direction. I only needed to go six or eight blocks. But finding my way in the whiteout was pretty tricky.

By the time I reached Mrs. Krauthammer's place, I was shivering uncontrollably. I can't tell you the feeling of relief that washed over me as I finally walked up the steps of her front porch.

The relief died pretty quickly, though. The front door was open. The glass in the door was smashed. And several pieces of furniture in the living room were overturned. My heart sank and a sick feeling ran through me.

"Mom!" I screamed. "Mom, where are you? Mom, are you okay?"

There was no answer.

I noticed that the back door of the house was open. I ran through the living room and into the kitchen. Outside in the snow I could see footprints. Whose were they? I figured I'd better follow them.

I went back inside, ripped off my ruined parka, grabbed a long wool coat off the coat tree by the door, and headed into the snow. I figured Mrs. Krauthammer would forgive me for borrowing her coat. I planned to make a strong point of not running through any more burning buildings today, so it should be in perfect shape when I returned it.

Outside the footprints were already starting to blur as the snow drifted into them. I noticed a small round circle on the ground. I stooped over. It was red.

Blood.

My pulse quickened. It wasn't a lot of blood. So I guessed that was a good thing. If it was Mom, at least she wasn't bleeding that badly. But how were they moving her? She was in no shape to walk. There was only one set of prints. Whose were they? I tried to go as fast as I could.

As I plunged on in a half jog, I realized that the coat I'd borrowed wasn't ideal. It was really more of a fall-weight coat. I had never really warmed up after wearing the burned parka. I was still shivering. But I had to find Mom, Fabe, and Katie. So I continued to follow the footprints through the driving snow. Here and there I saw drops of blood, too.

Sometimes I would see a house or a street sign or a traffic light. But I didn't really pay attention to where I was going. I just followed the footprints. What I suddenly realized was that every step I took, the prints were getting harder and harder to see. They must have left quite a few minutes before me, so I was working against time.

Suddenly I lost them.

One minute there were prints on the ground. The next . . . nothing! Around me was a quiet world of falling snow. The wind had died down, so it was like being in some kind of soundless cocoon.

I tried to go in a circle and find where the trail took up again. The problem was, how do you make a circle when you can't see anything around you. I was pretty sure they were just covered by drifting snow or something. If I just could find the trail again . . .

Then I saw it. A footprint. I darted forward. For a moment I felt better. I was back on the trail again! Then I saw another bloody splotch in the snow. The blood was already frozen. This splotch was bigger than the other ones I'd seen.

I ran on, following the fading depressions in the snow. And stride by stride, I began to lose them.

This time I knew that there would be no circling around to find them again. Because they were simply fading away into nothing.

Still, I kept on. I had to stop jogging because it was just too hard to see. I started being like one of those Indian trackers in some lame old cowboy movie—bent over, peering at the ground. Here and there I could see just enough evidence that my friends had been this way that I could stay on the trail.

But finally it was no good.

The trail had simply disappeared. Gone. Nothing left.

I stood there in the snow. I couldn't see anything.

Just the clotted mass of dull gray flakes falling out of the dull gray sky. Around me, nothing but snow.

I realized that I hadn't seen a landmark in a long time. Not a tree, not a house, not a stop sign. Nothing.

The thing about Greenville is that it's really a very small town. Especially if you go north out of town, it doesn't take long for you to end up out in the country. And once you get there, you run out of landmarks in a hurry. Cornfields can run on for close to half a mile in each direction sometimes. You could get lost in the middle of one of them and wander around in circles for ages.

I stopped and listened, hoping to hear a sound that would help me—a car, a church bell, a pig grunting . . . anything.

But there was just nothing out there.

And then I heard something. A long pulsing howl.

A wolf.

I shivered.

The cry of the wolf faded away. And then there was nothing at all.

Once again, I had this strange feeling of total aloneness. Not just a feeling of being by myself, the kind of feeling you have when you're alone in a house at night or something like that. This was different. This was a feeling of being alone in the universe. It was like everything dropped away. School. Kids. Friends. Buildings. Trees. All of it. Gone.

For a minute I considered giving up. Not just giving up on finding Mom. But giving up on everything. Just letting it all go. Sitting down in the snow and waiting for whatever came next.

But then I thought, *Well, dude, that's totally dumb!* Was I seriously considering lying down in the snow and freakin' freezing to death? What a totally idiotic idea.

"Hey!" I shouted. "Hello! Anybody out there?"

I didn't move. I just waited silently.

And then I heard it. A distant cry, so distant it was almost lost in the muffling silence of the snow.

I ran toward the sound. Then I stopped.

"Hey!" I shouted.

"Hey!" This time the voice was clearer.

I ran again, then stopped.

"Hey! Are you out there?"

There was a moment of silence. For a terrifying moment I thought maybe I'd gone the wrong way and lost them. But then the voice called back. "Chass? Is that you? Chass?"

It was Katie. "Katester!" I shouted. "Where are you?"

"Over here!"

I ran toward her.

Then *boom,* we actually smashed into each other. We fell down in the snow, giggling. The dim light gleamed off the various piercings in her face.

"Thank goodness!" I said, hugging her.

We struggled to our feet, both of us grinning. I dusted the powdery snow off my coat. "So where's Mom and Fabe?" I said.

Her smile faded. She took off her mitten and rubbed her hand. There was a big gash on her arm. A drop of blood slipped off and fell into the snow, leaving a red mark in the snow about the size of a dime.

"I don't know," Katie said. "I don't know where anybody is."

# TWENTY

"I GUESS YOU'D been gone about twenty minutes," Katie said, "when it happened."

"When *what* happened?"

We were trudging back through the snow, following my own footprints. With Katie's sprained ankle, we weren't moving very fast.

Katie looked morosely at the gash on her hand, then put her mitten back on and rubbed her hands together hard. "How does somebody become a surgeon?" she said.

"Huh?" I said.

"I just keep thinking about what I did today. With your mom? I'm not trying to freak you out or anything. You'd think that cutting somebody's flesh and sewing them and reaching inside them with those forceps thingies . . . you'd think that would be like . . ."

"Horrifying?" I said. "Disgusting? Gross? Icky? Vomitaceous?"

"Vomitaceous, yeah," Katie said. "Whatever that is."

"But it wasn't."

Katie looked at me curiously. "Yeah. Yeah, it wasn't. I felt like this just . . . POW! Like, something had just . . . like the real me had just come smashing out of my chest." She patted herself all over her body. "It's like this person was always just—have you ever seen in a science-fiction movie where like there's this normal dude standing there and then like his skin starts cracking and this big monster comes out?"

"Does this have anything to do with what happened to Mom?" I said.

But Katie was patting herself, pulling at her coat, like it was something bizarre and unfamiliar. "That's how I felt, dude!" She had this odd little smile on her face. "Except . . . I felt like this person—me—this dork with all the pieces of metal sticking out of her face—I felt like *this* person was the monster. And the thing that came out of my chest was something beautiful. Like it was the real me."

"Um . . ."

"So I just keep thinking, like, how do you . . . how does some little hick weirdo like me ever get to be a surgeon?"

"You go to college, you go to medical school, you get a residency in surgery. Then you're a surgeon."

"Oh." She seemed lost in thought. "You know nobody in my family has ever graduated from high school? People like me . . ." Her voice died out. "My dad used to joke about how he's a graduate of Faribault University."

"I don't get it."

"Faribault is the state prison down near Minneapolis." Katie's voice was bright, brittle, like an icicle about to snap. I'd heard people make mean jokes about her family before. But I'd never known her dad was in prison. I was getting the impression there were a lot of things in her life that she didn't talk about. Maybe that's why we got along so well.

Our feet went *squonch squonch squonch squonch* in the snow.

"So, could you tell me what happened back there?" I said.

"Sorry." She *squonched* along some more, wincing at each step. Then she said, "It all happened so fast."

"Is Mom okay?"

"I don't know. Like I say. It happened fast." She took a deep breath. "I was in the bathroom. I heard a noise outside. An engine noise. Like a snowmobile. Then there was this loud smashing noise. And then people started yelling. So I just kinda . . . hid."

The footprints in the snow were starting to fade a little. It was still easy enough to see them. But I knew we were in a race against time again. If they faded before we found a landmark . . .

"I was so scared." Katie wiped at her face. "I'm sorry, Chass! I should have done something. But I was so scared! Then I heard shots. Somebody screamed. Then there was some thumping and bumping. I just hid there till the noise stopped."

"And then?"

"And then I came downstairs. And everybody was gone."

"Did you recognize any voices?"

"Well . . . I heard a man's voice. It sounded familiar. He goes, 'What do you know? What do you know?' And then there was this *boom boom!* And then the scream. And then thumping. And then nothing."

"Nothing at all? What about the snowmobile?"

*Squonch squonch squonch squonch squonch.*

"Yeah," Katie said finally. "The snowmobile started up again. And then it went away."

"And the voice? The man's voice? You said it was familiar."

She sighed loudly. "I . . . maybe."

"So it was somebody you knew?"

"I don't know! I don't know!" Katie was shaking her head like a boxer who'd just taken a nasty punch in the face.

"How'd you cut yourself?"

"Pushing open the front door to see if anybody was out there. I cut it on the broken glass."

"Oh. I followed the blood because I thought it was Mom."

My teeth were chattering now. I was starting to get worried about the cold. My toes and fingers were numb and my face felt all raw and hot, like somebody was pressing a hot iron against my skin. My footprints were starting to fade. And still we hadn't come across any landmarks. "We need to find someplace," I said.

"Yeah," Katie said.

Something kept rattling around in my brain. The name Elliot Krieghoff, the lawyer who had filed that paper to get Cale Van Epps committed to the loony bin.

"Elliot Krieghoff," I said. "Do you know what his dad's first name is?"

"Uh, *Mister* Krieghoff?"

"Be serious."

"Well, Elliot's name is Elliot Krieghoff Junior. So I'm taking a wild flying guess that his dad is named—"

"No kidding!" I said. I thought about it for a minute. "The voice you heard—could it have been Mr. Krieghoff?"

"I don't know. I just . . . I just feel like . . ." She sighed again. "I don't even know if I'd know his voice."

We kept *squonching* on, my footprints getting harder and harder to see. Just when I was afraid we'd be reduced to shouting into the void like I'd done earlier, Katie said, "Look!"

"Where?"

I looked where she was pointing. But I couldn't see anything. And then the snow slackened a little. Just enough that I could see a light for a brief moment. We ran toward it, me holding on to Katie as she hobbled awkwardly forward.

A big dark thing swam up out of the snow. And there it was—a house.

Katie ran up and banged on the door. A small girl opened it and looked out without speaking.

"Hi," Katie said brightly. "Is your mom or dad home?"

The little girl threw back her head. "Moooooommmmmm-meeeeeeeeee! There's a big girl here with rings in her face!"

A woman I didn't recognize appeared in the doorway. "I'm sorry to bother you, Mrs. Langford," Katie said. "But me and my friend . . . we're lost in the snow."

I didn't recognize the woman. But obviously Katie did. "My word! Katie! Come in, come in," Mrs. Langford said.

She let us in and closed the door.

"Mrs. Langford is the guidance counselor at the elementary school," Katie said.

"Oh, hi," I said. "I'm Chass. I just moved to Greenville. Thank you *so* much for letting us in. We're totally lost."

Within a few minutes Mrs. Langford was plying us with hot chocolate as we sat in front of a huge roaring fire.

"I can't tell you how much we appreciate this!" I said.

"Oh, it's nothing. You'd do the same for me if I got lost out there," Mrs. Langford said. She kept staring at me with this odd expression on her face—half sad, half curious. "So," she said finally. "I hear you've had a pretty awful day, dear."

I nodded. Now that I was sitting there in front of the fire, it was starting to sink in.

"Miss Hill was an extraordinary woman," Mrs. Langford said. "A real Renaissance woman. I believe she played every instrument in the band. Plus piano, guitar, harmonica . . . She was a stalwart of the Little Theater, too. She directed *Showboat* last year. She used to sing when she was younger—but she gave it up when she got older. And on top of that, she was very smart with numbers."

"Numbers?" I said.

"Oh yes. The school district is so small, they couldn't afford a full-time person to keep the books. I believe that officially she was supposed to teach three classes a day. And then the other half of her day, she was the accountant for the district. Imagine that! What a contrast."

"Did she ever do any work like that for Mr. Krieghoff?" I said.

"You mean like—"

"Like accounting, keeping his books or something."

She looked at me strangely. "I wouldn't know." She cocked her head. "I mean, that would seem awfully strange, wouldn't it?"

"I don't know," I said. "Why would it?"

"Well..." She squinted at me. "Well, of course, you wouldn't know, would you?"

"Know what?"

"Evangeline Hill was Elliot Krieghoff's first wife."

My eyes widened. "What!"

"Yes. He moved here back when I was a little girl in the sixties. He started out as a lawyer. Somehow he met Miss Hill. They had a torrid fling, flew off to Vegas or someplace, and came back married." She lowered her voice. "That marriage lasted about ten minutes! Back in those days it was quite scandalous. She changed her name back to Hill after the marriage was over." She frowned. "But you know... now that I think about it?

Yes, I believe she did work for him for a while. I'm sure he didn't have much money to pay for a secretary or a bookkeeper or anything like that. So she probably helped out in her spare time."

"So is he still a lawyer?" I said.

"I suppose he might still be a member of the state bar. But, no, he hasn't practiced law for years."

"Why did he stop being a lawyer?"

Mrs. Langford shrugged. "He didn't do criminal law. I guess he did wills and real estate and corporate thingamajiggies. I don't know much about law. But I can't imagine there was *that* much call for that sort of a lawyer around here back then. So after a while he bought the old hardware store and turned it into the Yamaha dealership. After that, he rented out his office building to Dr. Winterthorpe, the dentist. I guess that was the end of his law career. More money in Jet Skis and snowmobiles."

"Huh," I said.

"Excuse me, girls," Mrs. Langford said. "I've got cookies in the oven. I better make sure they aren't burning."

I watched her as she left, thinking about what she'd just said. *Wills. Real estate. Corporate thingamajiggies.* I wasn't sure what a corporate thingamajiggy was. But

I had a hunch that a paper that says *Trust and Indenture* at the top would come under the general category of "corporate thingamajiggy."

The phone rang and Mrs. Langford answered. I could hear her having a soft conversation. I tried to block it out so that I could think straight. Pieces were starting to fall together in my mind. I remembered the conversation I'd had earlier in the day with Mrs. Krauthammer. She said that after Kyle Van Epps's mother died, a letter came to a lawyer in Greenville instructing him to sell the farm. Was it Mr. Krieghoff? Probably.

I now knew that Kyle Van Epps didn't really own the farm. His brother, Cale, did. So he could only have sold the farm after getting Cale committed to the funny farm . . . and somehow getting control of Cale's money. I was pretty sure it would take a lawyer to do that, too. Maybe that's what that trust-and-indenture stuff was about. Suddenly I wished I'd been paying more attention when I was reading it to Mom.

The more I thought about it, the more I saw connections between Mr. Krieghoff and Miss Hill. What if she knew something about the connection between Elliot Krieghoff and Kyle Van Epps—something that she was threatening to tell people about?

Maybe she threatened him. Maybe she was going to blackmail him. So Elliot Krieghoff shot her.

He thought it would be the perfect crime, killing her in the middle of a blizzard. But then he realized he'd been seen. He recognized me, so he assumed I recognized him.

Then he saw Mom wearing the same hat I'd been wearing an hour earlier, so he shot her.

But then he'd questioned me at his house. When I told him I hadn't seen who shot Miss Hill, maybe he decided he didn't need to kill me. Or maybe he just didn't want to do it in his own house, where the crime might leave incriminating evidence. He figured he'd follow me and do it somewhere else.

I kept spinning out the possibilities. There were a lot of possible scenarios.

There was still a piece missing.

Shooting Miss Hill, that added up. Shooting Mom, that made sense, too, I guess. Burning Miss Hill's house, that probably made sense, too, knowing that she had all those papers in the basement. There must have been something incriminating there, something connecting Mr. Krieghoff to a crime . . . or to something so embarrassing he'd be willing to kill to cover it up.

But the one thing I couldn't figure out was—

Katie interrupted my thoughts. "You think Mr. Krieghoff did it?" she whispered.

I nodded. Then I explained everything that had been going through my head.

"Whoa!" she said. She looked thoughtful. "Yeah. Yeah, okay. That all makes sense." She frowned. "Except . . ."

"Except what?"

"Why would he burn down the school?"

I nodded. "Yeah. Why *would* he burn down the school?"

Katie stared fixedly into the fire.

"You're not thinking about this at all, are you?" I said finally.

"Huh?" Katie said.

Mrs. Langford hung up the phone and went into the kitchen.

"Mr. Krieghoff," I said. "Miss Hill. The murder. You're not thinking about them at all, are you?"

She started pulling studs and rings and stuff out of her face, tossing them into the fire.

"What are you doing?" I said.

"This isn't me anymore," she said. "Can you imagine a surgeon with all this crap sticking out of their face? Would you trust a person who looked like me to do surgery on you?"

It seemed a little premature to be worrying about that. But I didn't see any point in popping her balloon. Maybe she *would* grow up to be a surgeon. Hey, why not?

I stood up. "We gotta go," I said. "We gotta figure out this missing piece. Why did Mr. Krieghoff burn down the school?"

"How are we going to do that?"

I reached into my pocket and pulled out the CD. Scrawled across the disc with a Magic Marker were the words *GHS Accounts Backup #1*. "Remember?" I said. "He smashed all those CDs in the office at school. At the time we were thinking it might be Elliot. *Our* Elliot. Elliot Junior. We were thinking he'd smashed it to destroy the records of his grades in band class. But it must have been something else. Maybe if we can find out what's on this CD, we'll know what Mr. Krieghoff was hiding."

Mrs. Langford's voice came out of the kitchen. "Oh, poop!" she shrieked. "The cookies! They're all burned!"

# TWENTY-ONE

OUT IN SNOW World again. I swear it was worse than it had been all day, the wind really howling and no visibility at all.

Before we left, Mrs. Langford had given me some dry clothes and a heavy coat. Now I was plenty warm. But as the falling snow folded around me and Katie, I couldn't help wondering what had happened to Mom and Fabe.

"The thing I can't figure out," I said, "is that I didn't see any tracks in the snow. There were only two doors in Mrs. Krauthammer's house. There was nothing in the front. And yours were the only ones coming out the back."

"Yeah, but I waited in that bathroom for a good while," Katie said. "The others probably got covered by the falling snow."

"I guess so," I said. "I just wish I knew—"

"Look, if he'd shot them, they'd all be lying there bleeding all over the floor. Wouldn't they?"

I shrugged. Logically, she was probably right. But it did nothing to allay my fear.

Mrs. Langford had told us that there was a barbed-wire fence running along the road in front of her house. If we just followed the fence, she said, it would get us back downtown. And from there we'd be okay. We walked in single file, Katie in front, me behind, our right hands dragging on the top strand of wire, so we didn't lose our bearings.

After a minute my glove snagged on a barb. I had to stop to try and free it. But the fabric had somehow gotten twisted around the barb. I started wrenching on it trying to get it free. In the distance, a wolf howled. Then another. Then another. Then another.

*How many of those things are out there?* I wondered.

I tried to calm down and get my glove free without yanking so hard. It would be stupid to tear a giant hole in it in this weather. I was so intent on my task that I didn't notice that Katie had kept walking. Since she was in front, she hadn't seen that I was stuck. I could only see about thirty feet. Katie had disappeared.

"Katie?" I called, still fiddling with my glove. There was no answer.

"Kate?"

Suddenly I was feeling panicky.

"Kate!" I started wrenching on the glove again. "Hey, Kate? Katester?"

Relief flooded through me as I heard footsteps crunching toward me.

"Oh, thank goodness!" I said. "God, Katie, you about gave me a heart attack."

I still couldn't see her. But I could hear her getting closer.

"Katie, over here," I said.

The wolves howled again.

Then a man's voice spoke. "Wolves love this kind of weather," the man said. "It's perfect for their method of hunting. They separate the weak. In the snow, the herd never even knows the victim is gone."

Then the man appeared. It was Mr. Krieghoff.

"Get away from me!" I shouted.

Mr. Krieghoff looked at me curiously. "Got your hand stuck, hon?"

"Why?" I said. "What was she going to do? What did she have on you?"

"I don't have the slightest idea what you're talking about," he said. "Elliot told me he got a call from somebody who said you and the girl with all that metal in her face were trying to walk back to town from Mrs. Langford's. I came out to make sure you didn't get stuck out here."

"Huh?" I said.

"The snowmobile's back that way a couple hundred yards. I hit this stupid barbed-wire fence twice and decided I needed to go the rest of the way on foot. Be a little embarrassing to run over you gals and kill you when I'd come out here to save you."

"There's really no need to play Mr. Innocent," I said. "I know what you did."

"What did I do?"

"You killed Miss Hill."

Mr. Krieghoff stood there looking at me with this vaguely amused expression on his face. "Did I?"

"She knew something about you. Something about your connection to Kyle Van Epps."

"I don't have a connection to Kyle Van Epps." He stood closer, put his hand on my trapped arm. "Stop jerking around so I can get this thing free."

"Yes, you do have a connection," I said. "You filed the papers that let him steal his brother's inheritance."

"Steal?" Mr. Krieghoff said. "That's a strong word."

"What would you call it?"

"Cale Van Epps is a severely emotionally disturbed man. He was put through absolute and complete hell as a child. He's not a normally functioning guy. You're right—I did handle the paperwork that got him put away. Involuntary commitment, the will, some trust work, whatever. But I'll tell you something. Cale Van Epps has been taken care of as well as is humanly possible. I knew Kyle back when he was just a kid. He's kind of a creep. But he loves his brother. No joke, he's left no stone unturned when it comes to caring for his brother."

"Really." My voice was skeptical.

"In fact, yeah. In addition to being a little bit crazy, Cale Van Epps is a musical genius. Did you know that?"

"I did."

"Yeah, well, Kyle paid for a whole musical studio so that Cale could get out of the loony bin once every couple of weeks and record his songs. Frankly, I gotta think that poor guy would have died long ago if he didn't have that outlet. Cale's one of these *Rain Man*–type guys. He's not normal. All he cares about is music, music, music. He's got this one huge talent. But otherwise, he's like a four-year-old. He can't tie his own shoes, he can't walk, he can't carry on a normal conversation without saying something weird and inappropriate. But he can write a heck of a song."

"He's made millions of dollars! What's happened to it?"

"It's in what's called a trust. It's a legal arrangement that Kyle set up a long time ago to make sure that Cale's provided for. What do you think pays for that fancy facility down there in Brainerd? You think a place like that is free? I bet you the Forest Glen Clinic costs close to a quarter mil a year. I mean, Cale's sold a lot of songs, sure. But that place burns through a ton of money."

I wasn't sure if he was BSing me or not. It sounded plausible. But it was hard to know. "What about the inheritance? I saw the will. Cale got the whole farm. You're telling me that Kyle didn't steal it so he could buy Apex Records back in the sixties?"

Mr. Krieghoff's eyebrows went up. "Look at you! You are just a little Nancy Drew, aren't you?"

"Well? Answer the question."

Mr. Krieghoff had finally gotten my glove free. He stepped back and made a squeaky noise through his teeth. "Steal. Hm. No, *steal* is not the word I would use. He set up an investment trust. Cale is what is known as the beneficiary of that trust. Meaning the money is legally his. But day to day, Kyle is the trustee. Meaning, he decides what happens with it. Steal it? Nope. On paper, sure, Cale is fabulously wealthy. And it's all because Kyle is such a smart businessman."

"So the bottom line is that a guy who's locked up in a private crazy house against his will is also the owner of the second-largest media empire in the world."

Mr. Krieghoff put his gloves back on. "Yep."

"Cale owns it on paper. But Kyle *controls* it."

"Pretty much the size of it."

"I think Miss Hill was going to reveal this. I think that's why—"

"Sweetie, sweetie, sweetie, hey, time out." Mr. Krieghoff made a T with his hands like a ref in a football game. "Look, yeah, I set up those trusts and did all that legal work for him. But you know what? I hated practicing law. It's the dullest thing in the world. So the first chance I had, I bought up a few properties around town and stopped practicing law. I haven't spoken to

Kyle Van Epps in thirty years. And you know what? You might or might not like the way he got control of that money. But it was all one hundred percent legal, one hundred percent aboveboard, one hundred percent defensible. So why would I care if all that stuff went public? I could give a rip. Ancient history."

I had pretty much run out of things to say.

"But, hey, let's just say for the sake of argument that I did kill Evangeline Hill over all this ancient history. Okay, fine. Burning down her house? Okay, maybe she's got some papers there that I'd want to get rid of. Fine. But what about the high school? You telling me it's a total coincidence that both her house *and* the high school went up in flames? In the middle of the worst snowstorm in the past thirty, forty years?" He rolled his eyes. "Come on! Somebody torched the place to get rid of some kind of evidence. But what could there be at that school that would connect the dots between me, Evangeline Hill, and Kyle Van Epps? Hon, it doesn't make sense."

He turned his back on me and started trudging up the fence line.

"Your little friend with the nose ring is sitting on my snowmobile waiting for us," he said over his shoulder. "You coming or not?"

I stood there, my face flushed, feeling like an idiot. I mean, if he really wanted to kill me, surely he'd have done it by now. And everything he said made sense. If Cale Van Epps really was some kind of *Rain Man* guy, a severely disabled person with one freakish talent— then everything Kyle Van Epps had done sounded . . . well . . . reasonable.

Just as Mr. Krieghoff was about to disappear into the snow, I decided that I had to follow him.

"Okay, let's say you're right," I said, running after him. "Then who *did* kill her?"

"Oh, let's see," he said airily. "Not my son. He's too weak. Not her boyfriend. Because she doesn't have one. Not Cale. Because he's locked up in the funny farm. Plus driving a wheelchair in this weather's a real bitch."

"Look," I said. "Miss Hill works for Kyle Van Epps. She's the one who helps Cale record his stuff. She keeps records of Cale's earnings and all that kind of thing."

"So?"

"Well, maybe *he* killed her."

Mr. Krieghoff laughed. "Surely, you're joking."

"He killed his dad," I said. "Why not Miss Hill?"

"That's different. That old bastard deserved killing more than anybody on this planet. A guy who'd keep his own son locked up in a cage for nineteen years."

"What do you think you're doing with your own son?" I said.

Mr. Krieghoff turned and stared at me. "What are you talking about?"

"The Big Plan?" I said. "You think he wants that? That's a cage just as much as that grain silo was."

His eyes narrowed. "I love my son!" he shouted. "I just want what's best for him!"

"Do you?"

Mr. Krieghoff's face trembled and his skin reddened. "You have no right to talk to me like this."

"Hey," I said. "I'm just telling you what I saw. What I know."

Then I saw the shape of the snowmobile swimming up out of the snow.

"I thought you said Katie was here," I said.

Mr. Krieghoff looked around irritably. "She was," he snapped.

For a second I thought maybe he was acting, that he'd already killed her or something. But if he had, he was sure a good actor.

"Hey!" he yelled. "Kid!"

There was no answer.

"What's her name again?" he said to me.

"Katie!" I yelled. "Hey, Katie! Where'd you go?"

A wolf howled in the distance.

"Wolves!" Mr. Krieghoff said in a tone of disgust. "Up to me? I'd kill every stinkin' one of them."

"Katie?" I called again.

Mr. Krieghoff climbed slowly onto the snowmobile. "I did what I could. If your little friend with the metal in her face doesn't want my help, I'm not gonna sit here and freeze to death waiting for her. Get on."

I didn't move.

"So if it wasn't you or Elliot or Kyle Van Epps, then who did it?" I said.

"Eileen Osmund," he said.

"Who?"

"Paul Osmund's wife. I knew it the second it happened."

"Why?"

"Everybody thought Paul hated Evangeline. But he didn't. He was crazy about her. Imagine how Eileen must have felt about that. Living with that phony little shrimp all those years, and him still moping around about a gal that gave him the brush-off decades ago? I'd have wanted to kill her, too."

"You really think so?"

Mr. Krieghoff shrugged. "Hey, it's a theory. The state police'll come down and sort it out." He hit the starter button and the snowmobile roared to life. It was the fanciest snowmobile I'd ever seen, with this complicated toolbox on the back. The box had a shovel on the side, and a rifle rack and a big battery-powered lantern and a bunch of other survival gear. "You coming or not?"

I looked around. I noticed that the snow had let up. Not just a little, but a lot. It was vaguely unnerving to be able to see the horizon after being cocooned in falling snow for hours. Behind us, I could see Mrs. Langford's house. In front of us was the city water tower and the outlines of some of the buildings downtown. To my right, far, far across a field, at the top of a gentle rise, was a grain silo. It was tilted slightly, like the Leaning Tower of Pisa, and the roof had fallen in.

And there was a tree next to it. The tree was covered by snow. But the outlines of a weeping-willow tree were unmistakable.

"What's that?" I said, pointing.

Mr. Krieghoff sighed loudly. "Yeah, yeah, yeah, that's it. That's the place. That's where Old Man Van Epps locked that poor kid up."

The killer—whoever it was—had heard me on the phone earlier. They'd heard me say that there was a clue in the silo. In this weather they might not have gotten here yet. But eventually they would. I figured I'd better get up there and start digging. While I still had a chance.

"You know what?" I said. "Thanks for coming to pick me up. But there's something I need to do. Can I borrow that shovel?"

Mr. Krieghoff scowled. "You've borrowed everything else I own today. Why not that?"

I took the shovel off the rack. He roared off without looking back. I climbed gingerly over the barbed wire. By the time I'd gotten all the way over, Mr. Krieghoff was out of sight.

Which was when it hit me. Where had Katie gone? Now I could see all around us. Her footprints crossed the road and went into the ditch on the other side of the road. Where they abruptly disappeared.

*Huh?* I thought.

And then I saw a wall of falling snow scudding toward me in the distance. The whiteout was coming back.

"Chass!" With relief I recognized Katie's voice. She sounded a little scared.

I turned back toward the sound. She was rising up out of the ditch. But there was someone behind her. A man. His arm was wrapped around her throat, trying to drag her back down where they'd been hidden in the ditch.

It was Mr. Osmund.

"Where is it?" he shouted.

"What?" I said. I was feeling confused.

"You know exactly what I'm talking about."

I looked around helplessly. He must have put it all together. He'd heard me talking about the silo, about the clue buried there, the one that would connect Kyle to the murder of his father. And maybe somehow the clue up there would draw the line between that murder and Miss Hill. Maybe even between Miss Hill and Mr. Osmund.

What was I going to do?

"Come on!" Mr. Osmund said. "I'm out of patience."

The wind had picked up, flinging snow across the ground. The wall of falling snow was moving toward us like a great gray curtain.

And in front of the snow were five, six, seven creatures loping easily through the snow.

Wolves.

I looked toward the silo. It had to be close to half a mile away. A long way in this snow. I realized I wouldn't make it before the snow hit.

"It didn't have to be this way!" Mr. Osmund shouted. I saw the gun in his hand then, pressed against Katie's face. "This was all a terrible mistake! All you have to do is give me the—"

"Run!" Katie screamed. "Run!"

I looked toward the west. Greenville was gone. The trees to the west were gone. The curtain of snow overtook the wolves. The world was disappearing again. The wolves were gone. Then the road was gone—and with it, Katie and Mr. Osmund.

"But now it's too late!" Mr. Osmund's voice came out of the swirling grayness. "I have no choice!"

"Run!" Katie screamed again.

I heard the flat ugly smack of a gun going off. Katie screamed.

I took a bead on the silo on the hill in front of me. If I could just run straight ahead . . .

Then the snow hit me. And the silo, too, was gone.

I ran into the snow.

# TWENTY-TWO

**EVERYBODY WHO HAS** been to a birthday party for a five-year-old kid has played pin-the-tail-on-the-donkey. You get blindfolded and spun around. Then you're supposed to walk straight forward and pin a paper tail onto a picture of a donkey's butt.

I always wondered who thought that game up. I mean, a donkey's butt? I don't get it.

Sorry, I know, I'm getting off track. The point is, when you watch somebody play pin-the-tail-on-the-donkey, you'll notice they never walk straight forward. Even if you point them straight at the donkey's butt, they start curving as they go forward. For some reason, when you can't see anything around you, you can't keep track of what's straight and what's not. Our brains just don't work that way.

So as I was running through all that blinding snow, I had this sudden flash in my mind, a sudden recollection of this party I went to when I was five years old. I remembered that all the kids were curving around and bumping into things and pinning the donkey's tail pretty much everywhere *but* the donkey's butt. But then this one kid just walked straight forward and nailed it.

After it was over, I accused him of cheating. That was the kind of kid I was, you know? Little Miss Self-Righteous. He got all mad and swore up and down that he wasn't cheating.

"So how did you do it, then?" I asked.

"I closed my eyes," he said, sticking out his lower lip. "And then I just *believed*."

Isn't that weird? I've thought about that kid for a long time. I don't even remember his name. Or even what town it was in. Maybe Cheyenne, Wyoming? I'm not sure. He had that ash blond hair that most kids lose by elementary school, and these really blue eyes. He had squinched them down and stared angrily at me, his little blue eyes burning into me.

"I just *believed*," he had said again.

I don't know why it stuck in my mind over the years, but it did. I guess what the boy really meant was that he lost all uncertainty. He stopped questioning himself. He just said to himself, *There it is.* And then he went for it.

So that's what I did. I knew that I was aimed in the right direction when I first started running toward that ruined silo on the hill. So I just believed.

I huffed and puffed and headed straight for where I believed the silo to be. The shovel that I'd taken off Mr. Krieghoff's snowmobile was growing heavy in my hands. But I tried not to think about that. *Just* believe! I kept saying to myself. *Just* believe!

Because, putting aside the fact that Mr. Osmund was chasing me with a gun, the field I was running across was huge. Night was coming on. I hadn't eaten since breakfast. The temperature was dropping.

Basically the everything-that-can-go-wrong-will-go-wrong scenario.

If I veered off course and got lost in that field, freezing to death was a real possibility. Calling for help would only bring Mr. Osmund and his gun.

I had to get where I was going. And hope that Mr. Osmund got more lost than I did. So I kept moving forward as fast as I could in the deep snow. Which isn't easy. I mean, I'm not much of a runner to begin with. But I just kept believing and trying to run as straight as I could.

"Just believe!" I whispered. "Just believe! Just believe!"

And it was working. I thought. Until I crossed over a bunch of footprints. Two sets of them. That was when I realized that somehow I'd circled around and crossed over my own tracks. And Mr. Osmund's. So he was definitely right behind me. I felt a sense of defeat settle over me like a black cloud.

Sometimes just believing isn't enough. I was getting really tired now. I staggered on blindly through the lonely gray strangeness of Snow World.

The only thing that gave me any satisfaction now was that I knew who had killed Miss Hill. It was Mr. Osmund. That was totally obvious. And I knew it had something to do with the disc in my pocket. But other than that, I knew precious little.

And even if I did figure it out, was I going to survive the day?

All I could do was struggle on and hope I got somewhere. Then something hit me. What if I *intentionally* crossed my trail a few times? Mr. Osmund would have a hard time finding me. He wouldn't know which tracks to follow. And eventually I'd run into the fence. Surely I would . . . Right? And once I did, all I had to do was follow it. I was inside a huge, enclosed field now. If I followed the barbed wire—just like Katie and I had on the road, the wire eventually would lead me up to the top of the hill. The silo was at the tippy top of the hill. So once I found myself going down, I'd know I had reached the right place.

I started intentionally curving around. Once, twice, three times, I crossed over my own tracks. Occasionally I used Mr. Krieghoff's shovel to obscure one set of tracks or the other, hoping that the falling snow would cover the shovel marks and further confuse Mr. Osmund. And as I worked, my mood began to change.

My plan was working! The oldest of my tracks were already starting to grow a little dim as the snow continued to sift down. If I was lucky, Mr. Osmund might follow them around in circles for a long time before he realized I'd tricked him. And by then, he wouldn't know which tracks were his, which were mine. He'd be completely turned around. And by then—I hoped!—I'd be gone.

Suddenly I saw something in front of me. A few horizontal lines, barely visible in the snow. The fence!

I ran toward it, grabbed the wire, and began jogging with renewed energy. I knew to get all the way around the huge field could be as long as a mile. Even though the gloves Mrs. Langford had loaned me were a little thin and my shoes were wet—still, my coat was warm. I *would* get there. Without a doubt. So I ran.

And ran.

And ran.

It seemed like nothing changed, though. There was just the sound of my footsteps and the gray aloneness of Snow World and the fence running along beside me, disappearing off into nothingness in front of me.

And so finally I had to stop running. It was too hard, leaping through all that thick snow. I was getting overheated and out of breath. I stopped, leaned against the fence, took a breather. In Normal World, a mile's not that far. But this wasn't Normal World. This was Snow World. A mile in Snow World is a long, long way.

The minute I stopped moving, the feeling of being alone started to close in on me. I mean, I knew Mr. Osmund was out there somewhere. But he might as well have been a million miles away. I was in Snow World.

And in Snow World, there was nothing but the snow and me.

Your eyes start playing tricks on you in Snow World. I started seeing flashes of things in the snow. Elbows, knees, frozen faces—sticking up out of the snow in the corners of my vision. Then I'd whirl and look. And nothing would be there.

It was always the same face. Miss Hill, her eyes filling with snowflakes.

So I started moving again. I trudged on and on. Eventually the fence took a turn. Snow World started to slant a little. I was walking up a slow rise.

My mood lifted. Slightly. I knew I was heading in the right direction. When I reached the top, I'd be there.

But knowing that didn't make me feel *that* much better. Knowing I was going the right way wasn't the same as being there. I still had to get to the silo, get to whatever was there. If I could find that key—and then get home safely—I'd be able to tie up the whole mystery. Mr. Osmund to Miss Hill, Miss Hill to Kyle Van Epps. And whatever secret had connected them all these years.

And then I had to get back to town, find Mom and make sure she was okay.

The closer I got to the top of the hill, the more crazy my vision got. I kept seeing Miss Hill in my mind, her body lying in the snow. And everywhere around me, she seemed to be welling up out of the drifts.

I knew it wasn't real. But still. In Snow World, you start to lose the sense of what's real and what's not. There's so little to hold on to in Snow World.

And then, suddenly, I slipped in the snow. It took me a moment to realize why I'd lost my footing. I had expected the next step to be up. But it wasn't. It was down.

There was no way to tell from looking. In Snow World you can't see far enough to tell if you're walking up a hill or down. You can only tell by doing it. By *feeling* it. I stood, took a few more steps. Yes! I was definitely walking down again.

This had to be it! I'd reached the top of the hill. Which meant I couldn't be more than a dozen yards from the silo.

I looked around. There was only Snow World. No silo. No willow tree. No rotted house foundations. Just the snow.

I climbed over the fence, and then tried to figure out

what to do next. I'd already determined that just believing was not going to help me keep my bearings. Maybe that stuff worked on pin-the-tail-on-the-donkey. But it didn't fly in Snow World. Somehow I had to get away from the fence far enough to find the silo . . . without getting lost.

If all I had to do was to find the silo and get back, it would be no big deal. I could just go out a few yards, look around, then follow my tracks back, go down the fence eight or ten yards, and walk out again. Eventually I'd find the silo.

But the thing is, it would take a while to find whatever I was looking for. And if my tracks got covered while I was digging . . . well, I might get stuck in the silo.

I needed a visual bearing. Something that would still be visible after being snowed on for a while. If I'd had sticks, I could have stuck them in the snow. But I didn't.

The only thing I could think of was my coat. If I kind of propped it up in the ground, it would stick up far enough that I could see it. As long as I was digging, I would—hopefully—stay hot enough that I wouldn't freeze. I figured it was worth a try.

I walked five strides, turned around. I could still see

the fence. Barely. I took off my coat, set it on the snow in a clump. It stuck up a good foot off the snow. Perfect.

Was I freezing? Of course. I walked five more strides, turned. I could still see the coat. I walked five more strides, turned. The coat was gone. I was now coatless in Snow World. Not a good thing!

I followed my footsteps back, put my coat back on, walked back to the fence. Somewhere—not very far away—a wolf howled. Then another.

And suddenly I wasn't alone in Snow World. I was . . . but I wasn't. I felt my skin prickle. Time to hurry!

I moved five strides down the fence, repeated the same operation. Five strides out, drop the coat, seven strides out, look for the silo. Still nothing.

It took me five tries. The top of the hill was a lot longer than it had seemed from the distance.

But I finally did it. I found the silo where Cale Van Epps had spent the first nineteen years of his life. In Snow World, it didn't look like a tall round concrete structure. It was just a curved wall that rose up and disappeared. Where Snow World ended, so did the silo. I circled around it, looking for an entrance. The wall of concrete was spiderwebbed with cracks.

Big and heavy as the wall was, it looked fragile, like the whole thing might come down in a heap if you kicked it hard. I circled and circled. Finally there it was, a dark doorway, shorter than I was. I crouched down and walked in.

Above me there was enough light that I could barely make out the top of the silo, a faint circle of light hovering up there over my head. A row of iron rungs protruded from the concrete so that—if you were insane, for instance—you could climb up the inside of the silo. I hadn't really been paying attention to the wind until I came into the silo. But now I realized how hard it had been blowing. I felt a lot warmer.

On the floor lay heaps of snow. There were lumps underneath the snow. But what they were, I couldn't tell.

The song had said the clue was "buried where I lay my head." Maybe there had been some kind of bed or mattress or pallet here a long time ago. But now there was nothing visible but snow.

I began to notice a strange sound—a sort of tooth-gnashing noise, like someone grinding their teeth until they cracked. It came from all around me.

Then I realized what it was. A fifty-foot-tall wall is as big as the sail on an old sailing ship. The wind must exert literally tons of force against the silo. Back when it was first made, the wind probably didn't budge the silo at all. But now that it was old and had started to crack, every breath of wind was making the silo grind against itself. The thing was more or less eating itself to death.

I knew it had probably been sitting there for seventy-five years without falling down. But still. It was creepy. I couldn't help feeling like it might come down on me any second.

*Where should I dig?* I just wasn't sure. I started stomping around the ground, kicking snow, trying to see if there was anything on the floor that would indicate where—

And then I found it. A rusted wire spring poking up through the snow. I dug down with my shovel and found it. The remains of an ancient, cheap mattress. There was nothing left of the stuffing. Just the springs. I dragged them away, leaving a rectangular grid in the snow.

*Where would he have laid his head?* I stared, trying to think. The farthest spot from the door was likely to be the warmest, right?

There. I couldn't know for sure. But I could guess. I picked what seemed the right spot. Then I started jamming my shovel down into the snow. There was a solid thunk as I hit the frozen dirt or rotted corn or whatever it was that lay in the bottom of the silo. I scraped away the snow until I found what was beneath it. Maybe it was dirt, maybe it was ancient rotted corn. Who knows? Whatever it was, it was solid as a rock.

And that's when the fun part started. Digging in frozen ground is just about the hardest, most frustrating thing imaginable. If you've ever tried to scoop really, really hard ice cream with a plastic spoon, you have an inkling of just how much it sucks.

You don't really *dig* frozen ground. You chop it. You stab it. You beat it. You whack it. You cuss at it. You chop it some more. You cuss some more.

I mean, I'm not big on cussing. I'm not one of those people who thinks that having a potty mouth makes you cool. But there are moments. There are words that were invented specifically for use when digging in frozen dirt.

And let me tell you, I used every one of them. Several times.

Then I heard the howl of the wolves again. Closer, this time. *Lots* closer. At which time I decided, *You know what? Maybe I'll shut up now.* I just kept chopping and hacking away at the ground, hoping that I was actually digging in the right place.

After a while I stopped and looked up. A few minutes earlier there had been a halo of light up above me. Now it was a halo of grayish dimmish vague-ish sludginess.

Which meant night was coming on. I *had* to get this done. Fast.

My hands were blistered. My back was sore. I couldn't feel my toes or my nose anymore. But I kept going.

And then there was a metallic thud. I'd hit something. I squatted down to look. But it was so dim now that I couldn't make out anything at all.

So I stood up and kept hacking at the frozen earth, hacking away until suddenly I felt the corner of something under my shovel. I took off my glove, reached down, felt around.

A box.

It was a small metal box.

I kept digging and prying, trying to get it to come free. With every passing minute I was getting more and more discouraged, more and more tired, more and more blind. It wasn't quite night yet—but the heavy clouds and snow were blotting out whatever sunlight might have been left in the day.

I took another brief rest, trying to catch my breath.

The one thing I could positively say was that I didn't miss my coat. In fact, other than my toes and my face, I was burning up, sweat dripping through my clothes.

With my last strength, I plunged the shovel into the frozen dirt, yanked the shovel hard—and something gave. The whole box had just shifted below me.

I reached down, grabbed it, picked it up.

"Yes!" I was so excited that I forgot about the wolves, forgot about Mr. Osmund, forgot about any need to be quiet. I just shouted. "Yes! I did it!"

My voice echoed hollowly around the silo.

Then I heard a scraping noise. For a second I thought it was the silo grinding and cracking under the force of the buffeting wind.

But it wasn't.

"Did what?" a voice said.

I looked up. And there in the murky light, I saw a man. Mr. Osmund.

"Nothing," I said, dropping the box on the floor.

Mr. Osmund didn't seem to see the box. His eyes were pinned on my face.

"Chass, Chass, Chass," he said, sighing. "Why did you and your snoopy mother have to come to this town?"

I took this to be a rhetorical question. So I didn't

answer it. I just tried to ease a little bit of snow onto the box with my foot.

"I mean, why not Rossburg? Why not Malmo? Why not Breezy Point or Waukenabo?"

"You know how many times I've thought that exact same thing today?" I said. "Why not Waukenabo? I bet Waukenabo is just a great town."

I moved a little to my side. I figured babbling like an idiot might distract him. I shifted some more snow with my left foot, pushing it up on top of the small metal box.

He shook his head sadly. "Miss Hill was always such a . . ." Mr. Osmund seemed to be in some pain, his face tight and drawn. "Miss Hill was always such a Goody Two-shoes. She always felt like she had to put her nose in where it didn't belong."

"What does this have to do with Kyle Van Epps?" I said. I eased a little more snow over the box. I was afraid to look down. I just had to hope he wouldn't notice it.

"What?" Mr. Osmund said sharply.

"Kyle Van Epps," I said again.

He looked at me like I was speaking Japanese. "What are you talking about?" he said sharply.

I didn't say anything.

He reached toward me, snapping his fingers. "Give it to me," he said softly.

"Give you what?" I said. I wasn't sure if he'd noticed me covering up the box or not. I figured I still had to play out my hand and play dumb.

"Don't act stupid," he said. "Just give it to me."

I shrugged and did my big ol' innocent puppy-eyes face. "I really don't know what you're talking about." I stepped away from the box, hoping to keep him from looking down at it.

He took a step toward me. As he did, he staggered slightly, like he was tired. Or even drunk. "No more . . ." He took a long, ragged breath. "No more Mr. Nice Guy."

There was a long silence. Even the wind had died down. Then I heard a soft noise. *Plop. Plop. Plop.* Something dripping into the snow.

I looked down to see where it was coming from. And then I saw what it was. Blood. There was blood dripping from his left arm onto the ground.

"That stupid old lady!" he said angrily. "She shot me!"

"Mrs. Krauthammer?"

"Mrs. Krauthammer." He took another breath. He

held out his hand. The blood on his hand looked like ink puddling up in his palm. "Just give it to me."

"Or what?" I said.

Mr. Osmund sighed. "You think I wanted it to end like this?"

"I don't know," I said.

"People look at me," he said. "They look at me and they see some little nobody. I know that. But I have my feelings. I have passions. I have—" He stopped, coughed, hand over his mouth. When he took his hand away, there was a drop of blood on his neat little mustache.

"Playing cards makes me feel alive." He waved his hand around. "So I got a little behind. Just a little. I had to borrow some money. It's not stealing. I was just borrowing it."

"What?" I said.

"Oh, but Miss Hill wouldn't understand that. She was too pure, too perfect!" His voice was soft, but spiteful. "She found the missing money and—oh, brother— she just hit the roof!"

"Missing money?"

"Don't play stupid. You know exactly what I'm talking about. I bet your mother's with the state police. Isn't she? Huh? Yeah? I bet she's an undercover operative." He laughed loudly. "What about you? I bet you're not even her daughter. Are you one of those young-looking cops, fresh out of the academy? Like in that movie a few years back, the one where they send that cop into a high school as an undercover narcotics agent? Huh? I always thought you were just way too mature acting."

"What are you *raving* about?" I said. I glanced down. One tiny corner of the box was still sticking out of the snow. I slid a little blob of snow over it. And the box was gone.

Mr. Osmund didn't seem to be paying attention to me. He sat down on the floor next to the door. "I just *borrowed* the money. I kept telling her, 'I'm going to pay it back.' But she wouldn't listen."

Now that I had covered the box up, I finally started paying attention to what he was saying. "Hold on, hold on," I said. "So none of this had anything to do with Kyle Van Epps?"

"Van Epps?" Mr. Osmund stared at me. "Why do you keep talking about—"

"Wait, let me get this straight," I said. "You lost some money gambling. You owed more money than you could pay to whoever you owed money to. So you borrowed money from the school bank account? Is that right?"

"Like you don't know this!" He spat on the ground. Where he spat there was a black spot. More blood. "The school district has a general fund. It's been in surplus for over nine years. The money sits there in the bank, no use to anybody. So I made a withdrawal. Ten thousand dollars. Sounds like a lot. But I had funds due on an investment. I knew the money was coming. I repaid it all. Every penny of it. But you couldn't forgive me, Evangeline! It wasn't according to procedure! It wasn't according to the rules!" He was waving his gun at me like he was talking to Miss Hill, not to me.

I didn't move or speak.

"Oh, you had to play by the rules! You were going to report me to the school board! I was three months from retirement, Evangeline! Don't you have any mercy at all in you? Don't you have any compassion? I would have lost my pension, Evangeline. They would have fired me and taken everything. Everything! All these years I've put in trying to help these ungrateful kids . . . and you had to rob me of everything!"

"It wasn't me, Mr. Osmund," I whispered. "I didn't do anything to you."

He blinked. Suddenly it was clear he was looking at me again—not some imaginary version of Miss Hill. "But you knew. Didn't you?"

I shook my head. "I didn't know anything."

"You're a liar." Suddenly his face twisted with anger. "You're a filthy little liar. I called the school you were supposed to have transferred from. They'd never heard of you."

I looked at the ground.

"So it made me curious. I looked into your mother's job references. It's not hard to find information like that in a little town. Not when you're a trusted figure like me." He smiled a twisted, bitter little smile. "It was all bogus. The references, the names, the phone numbers. Your mother doesn't even exist."

"Okay, but—"

"Liar!" He stabbed the gun at me. "Liar. Liar."

"You know, Mr. Osmund, I've lied about a ton of stuff in my life. You're right. Mom and I are not who we say we are. But we're not with the freakin' state police, I'll tell you that much!"

"Liar!"

"I'm not lying!" Suddenly I felt this weird need to prove I wasn't lying. I don't know why. It was like I was more worried about proving I was right than I was about saving my life. Weird. But that's how I felt.

"You're lying, Chass. Or whatever your name is. Why else would you have taken that accounting disc?"

"Accounting disc?"

"I saw you! Don't lie to me. When you came out of the building you had a CD-ROM in your hand. One of the backup discs for the school computer. Apparently I failed to destroy one of them this morning. I was in a bit of a hurry. As you might imagine."

"Accounting disc," I said. Then my eyes widened. "I thought it was grades. I took it because I thought it had Elliot Krieghoff's—" I broke off. "You want *this*?" I said, reaching into my pocket. Then I realized that it was in the pocket of my coat. Which was lying in the snow.

"It's outside," I said.

"Where?"

"In my coat."

"Oh," he said. He started pushing himself to his feet. "You wouldn't lie to me."

I shook my head.

"Good," he said. "Because I really need that disc. Without that disc, nobody can prove anything."

"Then you can let me go," I said. "I mean . . . if I can't prove anything . . ."

Mr. Osmund sighed wearily. "I wish that were the case. Heartily, I do." He lifted the gun toward me. His hand was shaking. I took a step backward. My hand hit something hard. One of the metal rungs that were sticking out of the concrete.

I looked up. You almost couldn't see anything up at the top of the silo anymore.

I knew what I had to do.

Outside, a wolf howled. It seemed very close now.

I turned and started climbing up the rungs of the ladder. One foot after another.

"Wolves," Mr. Osmund said softly. "They live in a different world, don't they? No lies. No truth. No honor. No responsibility. It must be so simple for them. The hunt, the chase, the kill, the meal. Back to the den for sleep. It must be nice, huh?"

I'd gotten maybe ten rungs up, when he fired the first round. It missed, hit the concrete near my shoulder. A few chips of concrete flew out and hit me in the face.

"I'll be the first to admit, I'm not the best shot," he said. "But I'll hit you eventually. And if I don't? Well, you don't have a coat on. You'll freeze inside an hour."

He fired again. Another miss. I could actually hear the bullet passing by my ear. It made a sort of sizzling snap. I kept climbing. Another shot. Then another.

"Can you imagine the feeling they must have?" he said. "Tracking their spoor through the wild darkness?

Hm? The blood trail, the smell of their prey in their noses? It must be amazing."

Another shot. This time it wasn't even close.

For the first time I looked down. I was amazed at how high I was. No wonder he couldn't hit me. He was nearly invisible now.

Then I saw something detach itself from the dark patch where the door to the silo was. A smear of motion in the darkness.

"What—" Mr. Osmund's voice was cut off by a loud thump.

Then he screamed.

The bottom of the silo seemed to boil—a strange dark tangle motion. For a moment I couldn't make sense of it. And then I realized.

Wolves. They growled and tore at him. It didn't last more than a few seconds. His screams subsided. There was some snarling and snapping as the wolves fought among one another. Then there was a soft scraping sound. They were dragging him away.

They must have followed the trail of his blood. Just like he said—trailing the spoor through the snow, the smell of it in their noses.

I clung to the ladder and waited.

# TWENTY-THREE

**WHEN I FINALLY** came down, I came down to a new world.

A bright moon hung over the white fields. The sky was a clear deep black, punctured by the brightest stars I'd ever seen in my life.

The world gleamed—pure and stainless and pale.

Mr. Osmund was gone. The wolves were gone. In the distance I saw the lights of Greenville winking cheerfully in the night.

I was shaking so hard that I could barely stand. My coat was right where I'd left it. I picked it up, put it on, slid Cale Van Epps's small metal box into the pocket—next to the CD that had caused so much tragedy today.

I surveyed the place where Kyle Van Epps's life had begun. It looked like the most peaceful place in the world. Then I turned and began the walk back toward town.

# TWENTY-FOUR

**WHEN I GOT** home, Fabe answered the door. He grinned and said, "She's here!" over his shoulder. I gave him a hug, then walked in and found Mom lying on the couch. She looked a little better than she had earlier.

"Oh, thank God!" she said, pushing herself up on one elbow. "I was so worried!"

"*You* were w-w-worried?" I said. I was shivering so hard I stuttered when I talked. "I wasn't the one who got shot and then suddenly disappeared from Mrs. Krauthammer's house."

"Oh, sorry about that. There was an intruder. He had a hood and snowmobile goggles on, so we couldn't tell who it was. Mrs. Krauthammer scared him off with the shotgun. We were afraid he might come back. So we left in somewhat of a hurry. In the confusion and the snow and everything, we got separated from Katie."

At the mention of Katie, I burst into tears. "I don't know what happened to her. I'm afraid she got shot."

The door to the bathroom opened and Katie was standing there. "Shot?" she said. "No, as you were running off, Mr. Osmund got distracted. I pushed him down and then ran off into the snow. His gun went off, but he didn't hit me. I don't even know if he was trying to shoot me. After that, I just followed the fence home." She, too, burst into tears, ran over, and hugged me. "I thought he was going to kill you!"

"He sure tried," I said.

I told them about everything that had happened that night, about how Mr. Osmund got attacked by wolves, about the box I'd found in the silo.

Then I set the small, rusted metal box in the middle of the coffee table.

Mom said, "So what's in it?"

"I haven't even looked," I said.

Everyone gathered around the table. I hadn't really gotten a good look at the box. It was a small metal case about half the size of a cigar box. Something clunked inside as I moved it around. The case was rusted with age. It was locked.

Fabe took out a pocketknife and handed it to me. "Pry it open," he said.

I slid the blade of his knife under the lid. It hardly took any pressure at all to pop the ancient lock open. Inside were several black-and-white photographs, so stained and faded as to be hardly recognizable. In one there was a small blond boy, grinning broadly at the camera, his eyes full of innocent enthusiasm. Even though he was probably fifty years younger than the man I'd met, I recognized him. It was Kyle Van Epps.

In the next photograph was a beautiful, sad-looking woman dressed in clothes that must have been unfashionable even back in the fifties when the picture was probably taken.

"Opal," Mom said. "His mother."

There was nothing else in the box. Nothing but a small, intricately cut key.

Mom stared. "That's *it*?" she said.

"That's it."

She picked up the key. "This? We risked our lives for two pictures and a key?"

"Maybe it's a key to something important," I said.

"Looks like a safe-deposit box," Fabe said.

Outside the house a snowplow rumbled by. Katie looked out the window. "The roads are getting cleared off," she said. "I'll be able to drive home."

I saw that Mom had heard the snowplow, too. And I knew what she was thinking. "We don't have to leave here, Mom," I said. "Miss Hill's murder had nothing to do with Kyle Van Epps. There's no need for us to leave town."

Mom didn't say anything for a minute. Finally she dropped the key back in the little box. It clinked and clattered.

I picked it up. "Wonder what it goes to?"

She sighed then rolled her eyes. "Well, I guess we'd better find out."

# TWENTY-FIVE

**THE NEXT DAY** there was a knock on my door. I opened it and there was Mrs. Osmund. She had a bundt cake in one hand. "I just thought I'd bring this over for your mother," she said.

"She's sleeping right now," I said.

Mrs. Osmund handed me the cake. I stood there for a minute. Mrs. Osmund didn't move.

"Would you like to come in?" I said.

She smiled a horrible grimace of a smile, then came

in and sat on the couch with her knees tightly clenched together.

"I talked to the state police this morning," she said. "I understand that you were the last person to see Paul alive."

I nodded.

"Eaten by wolves!" she said. "In America. How is that even possible?"

"I'm sorry," I said.

"Did he suffer?"

"It was over very quickly," I said.

"They still haven't found his body," she said.

"They dragged him off," I said. "I'm sure they'll find him soon. When all the snow melts."

Mrs. Osmund shuddered and a tear ran down one side of her face, dripped off her chin.

"Is there anything else?" I said.

She looked around for a moment. "You didn't tell them," she said finally.

"Tell them what?" I said.

Mrs. Osmund gave me that grim smile again. "He wasn't really working on his cuckoo clock that morning. I guess you knew that."

I shrugged.

"Paul told me everything. He wasn't a dishonest

man, you know. Before he came after you, he told me you'd found something. A disc?"

I didn't say anything.

"You know," she said, "he spent all our savings on his gambling habit. All that I'll have to live on is his state teacher's pension. If they decide he stole that money from the school district, they'll take that away, too."

"I figured that," I said.

She sat quietly, hands folded, knees still tight together, like she was afraid some boy might suddenly burst into the room and look up her skirt.

I reached into the pocket of my coat, pulled out the disc, and handed it to Mrs. Osmund.

"I'm not going to lie to them," she said. "If they come and ask me for it, I'll give it to them." She paused, fingered the hem of her coat. "But if they don't ask . . ."

"Okay," I said. I could have told her a lot about lying to protect yourself. I wasn't going to pass judgment.

"Why didn't you tell them?" she said. "When you talked to the state police? You could have told them that he was the one who killed Miss Hill. You could have told them everything."

"I talked to Mom last night before the state police got here. She figured that if I told them what really happened, you'd be left without any future. Miss Hill didn't have any family, didn't have anybody who needed to know the truth. So what's to gain? It's not your fault what he did."

"Well. Thank you for that."

We sat in silence for a long time. Finally I said, "Is there anything else?"

"Wolves," she said. "Was it really wolves? I mean . . . if you shot him or something? To protect yourself? I wouldn't blame you."

I shook my head. "It was really wolves," I said.

"Wolves." She had a blank look on her face.

"Wolves," I said. "Right here in Minnesota. Go figure."

Finally she stood up and smoothed down the front of her coat. Then she eyed the cake uneasily. "I'm not a very good baker," she said. "It's just out of a box."

"That's okay," I said.

She looked like there was something else she wanted to say. But she didn't. She just opened the door and walked outside. It was almost fifty degrees and the snow was already melting.